Kathleen James has put her practical side away for once and looks forward to the perfect romantic evening: an intimate dinner with the man of her dreams—and an engagement ring. She is not prepared to hear that he wants to bring his grandmother back from Italy to live with him.

Dominic Lawrence has planned this marriage proposal for six months. Nothing can go wrong—until his Nonna calls. Now he must interrupt the tenderest night of Katie's life with the news that another woman will be under their roof.

When Antonia's sister dies, she finds herself longing to be back in the states. An Italian wartime bride from the '40s, she knows how precious love can be. Can her own story of an American soldier and a very special collie once again bring two hearts together at Christmas?

PRAISE AND AWARDS

"Aubrey Wynne creates a character that's easy to fall in love with..."
~Kishan Paul, author of Blind Love and Second Wife

Winner of Preditor and Editors Reader's Choice
Short Story Award:
Merry Christmas, Henry

"Captivating Christmas Choice!"
~Kindle Book Review

Winner of Preditor and Editors Reader's Choice
Short Story Award:
Pete's Mighty Purty Privies 2014

"Expertly written and hysterical. You can't go wrong with this one!

~Renea Mason, author of Symphony and Light and The Good Doctor series

Dante's Gift
"...a really beautiful love story that will touch everyone's heart and brings tears to your eyes."
~Winnie Lim, Goodreads Review

OTHER BOOKS BY AUBREY WYNNE

Dante's Gift
(A Chicago Christmas novella)

Merry Christmas, Henry
(A Chicago Christmas novella)

Pete's Mighty Purty Privies
A Just for Sh*#$ and Giggles Short Story)

To Cast A Cliche
(A Just for Sh*#$ and Giggles Short Story)

DANTE'S GIFT

(A Chicago Christmas Book #1)

By

AUBREY WYNNE

ISBN-13: 978-1-946560-11-7

ISBN-10: 1-946560-11-1

Editing by The Editing Hall and Patricia C. Zick

Cover   Art   by   Syneca Featherstone

Formatting by Anessa Books

DEDICATION

To my sisters, Mindy and Katie, who support me in everything I do, as good sisters should. And to my stepfather and British WWII veteran, Eric Merry, for his invaluable help with the WWII background. At ninety-two, his memory is better than mine.

ACKNOWLEDGMENTS

Much love and appreciation to my mother and editor, from whom I inherited the "writing gene." Thanks again to my muse and sister, Mindy, who fixed the opening and always brainstorms with me over a bottle of wine. My beta reader Julie Fowler who read this story multiple times and insisted it was just as good each time. And a special to hug to my divas, Valerie Twombly and Kishan Paul. Valerie, you are ever the voice of reason and common sense. You have taught us so much. Kishan, you are the sweet whisper of support and gentle nudge that keeps me going.

Love is friendship that has caught fire. It is quiet understanding, mutual confidence, sharing, and forgiving. It is loyalty through good and bad times. It settles for less than perfection and makes allowances for human weaknesses.

Anne Landers

CHAPTER ONE

The piles of discarded clothes resembled the glorious Chicago skyline at dusk. The deep sunset colors cluttered the floor and the bed, as Katie James systematically emptied out the huge walk-in closet. She shook her head in frustration each time she gazed at the mirror in a new outfit.

This was *the* night. The night Dominic would pull a dazzling ring from his pocket and ask her to become his wife. He had been like a kid with a big secret for the past three weeks: distracted, smiling for no apparent reason, and cracking stale jokes. All sure signs that he plotted with the "happy gods." Several times when she'd texted or called, he told her he was Christmas shopping. Ha! No man bought holiday gifts in October. He said to dress up because he had something special planned. There could be only one explanation—a proposal.

Looking out the window from her Lake Point Tower condo, she watched the sailboats bob in Lake Michigan and played out the evening in her mind. Dominic would be dressed in a tailored suit that hugged his wide shoulders. His long fingers would betray his nervousness as they combed through his thick, dark wavy hair. She would shiver delicately when those smoky eyes caressed her face. He would reach for her hand—

Good grief, get a hold of yourself. This is real life not some sappy chick flick.

Jasmine, her best friend, plopped onto the couch. "What are you wearing tonight? I came to give my approval. I have a better sense of romance than you."

"What's that supposed to mean?"

Her friend snorted. "You create ledgers while I create romantic allusion."

"True, I could use another opinion. My room looks like a tornado hit it. I'll pour you a glass of Merlot and put on a fashion show."

An hour later, both women stood in front of the full-length mirror with huge grins. Katie turned from side to side, watching the vibrant jade dress sway under the black silk jacket. A hint of cleavage peeked out from the scooped neckline. "You are brilliant. I would have never put this together."

"That's why I design clothes and you add numbers. See how the darker colors showcase that deep auburn hair?" Jazzy said as she arranged the mass of waves into a loose chignon, leaving long curls to frame her oval face. "I wish you would show more leg, but this is subtly sexy. Now where are the green topaz earrings and pendant your parents bought you last Christmas? They're the exact color of your eyes."

An hour later, after a professional make-up session, she gave her friend a hug. "Good luck tonight. I hope it's everything you have dreamed of since we were girls."

Katie laughed. "No, you hope it's everything *you* have dreamed of since we were young. "

"Same thing. I admit I always thought I'd find my soul mate first, though."

She rolled her eyes. "You know I don't believe in that. Love, yes. True love, love at first sight, fate? No. Compatibility, similar backgrounds and interests, friendship—those are the things that determine lasting love."

"Yeah, yeah, yeah. But you can't tell me your stomach never flips when he looks at you a certain way, or your legs get wobbly during a particularly passionate kiss." Jazzy waggled her finger and ignored the second roll of eyes. "Now remember to get at least a little teary-eyed when he pops the question. Pinch yourself if you have to but let him know how much this means to you. We both know you're lousy at saying what you feel."

"You make me sound like a cold fish," she said with frown. "I don't ooze emotion but I can show affection. Besides, I didn't have much practice in my family."

"When was the last time you gave me a hug?"

"Just now." Katie bit her lip, knowing what was next.

"No, I hugged you. There's a difference. I'll get off my soapbox if you promise to try to make tonight as special for Dom as he is making it for you. Throw sensibility to the wind and kiss him in public." She headed for the door. "And for god's sake, don't forget to tell him you love him. He should not have to take it for granted when he puts a ring on your finger."

"Time out! I promise to wear my heart on my sleeve and follow all the rules of Miss Jasmine's School of Romance, if you promise to leave now," she agreed and pushed her friend toward the door. "Go pretend you hate Thomas and leave me in peace. I'll call you first thing in the morning."

"Call me from the bathroom afterwards. I want to know all the details."

Katie shut the door. From the other side came a muffled, "And text me a picture of the ring."

A few minutes later, Vivaldi's Four Seasons played on her cell phone. Dom's handsome face smiled up at her, and she quickly swiped the screen. "Hey there. Not cancelling on me, are you?"

"Not a chance. Finished up the week's orders and cleared some days on next month's calendar." He paused then continued in a low, caressing tone, "I miss you, Kathleen James. It's been a week since I've held you in my arms. No more extended business trips if you want me to remain a gentleman."

Her pulse raced as his deep voice flowed through her like a rich cup of coffee. "Don't threaten me, Mr. Lawrence. You're the one working twelve-hour days. Besides," she added, getting into the spirit of the game, "maybe I like an old-fashioned rogue once a in awhile."

The moan on the other end made her chuckle. "Are you still picking me up at seven?"

"What time is it now?"

"Grrr. It's six-fifty." She tapped her foot on the hard wood floor. "You're late again, aren't you?"

"Is that your toe making a staccato beat? I-am-ir-ri-ta-ted. Why-can't-he-be-on-time." She could hear the grin in his tone. *Sense of humor, check.*

"You took the words right out of my—" A knock at the door. "Hang on a minute, okay?"

Not expecting anyone, she looked through the peephole. A charcoal-grey eye stared back at her. She quickly opened the door.

"Boo!" He held out a bouquet of white and pink flowers.

The aroma of white roses and star lily gazers filled the room. *Thoughtful, check.* Then he pulled her close, nibbling at her lips as her arms went around his neck. When the kiss deepened, the flowers fell to the floor. Katie leaned into him, allowing his strong hands to hold her up.

Strong and sexy. Check.

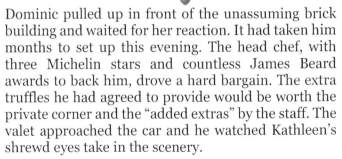

Dominic pulled up in front of the unassuming brick building and waited for her reaction. It had taken him months to set up this evening. The head chef, with three Michelin stars and countless James Beard awards to back him, drove a hard bargain. The extra truffles he had agreed to provide would be worth the private corner and the "added extras" by the staff. The valet approached the car and he watched Kathleen's shrewd eyes take in the scenery.

"No way. You have tickets to dine at Alinea's?" She shook her head. "Do you know how much—"

He put a finger on her mouth, then brushed the long, red curls from her cheek and put his lips in their place. "You are so beautiful... let me spoil you tonight without one word about the price."

She smiled and kissed him back, her lips soft against his skin, then wiped her lipstick print off with her thumb. The valet opened the door and he ducked his head as he climbed out of the silver Lexus. He walked around to the other side and assisted his beautiful date onto the sidewalk.

The restaurant, tucked away on Halsted, occupied what had once been a residential brickstone. They entered a long, darkened hallway strewn with hay and pumpkins for the season and passed a very busy kitchen. He tightened his grip on Katie's arm before she gravitated toward the commotion and smells. A pleasant younger woman greeted them and escorted them upstairs to a secluded corner.

"I didn't expect this décor to be so minimal. I imagined a few priceless paintings on the wall or chandeliers." She nodded in approval at the sand-colored walls with dried arrangements of reds and yellow and oranges for accents. "I love it."

Dom explained, "Most people expect lavish because of their reputation, but the philosophy is to focus your attention solely on the food." A waiter appeared with the first wine selection. "And the beverages." He gave his approval for the first bottle by a slight incline of his head.

With the first course of shrimp, clams in their shells, and seaweed, the server asked to imagine a beach; the small shrimp washing ashore among the seaweed and seashells. Dominic could almost hear the ocean.

The next two hours produced a display of mesmerizing dishes with a production and story to accompany each course. He stopped counting after ten and lost himself in the experience. The gorgeous redhead next to him lit up with each new presentation and kept her promise. She never once brought up the $600-$800 plates.

During a hot potato-cold potato course, the waiter leaned down and said softly, "The head chef said he is especially pleased with the black truffles. He hopes you will come again soon."

"Tell him if he has done his job, I won't need a return visit." He looked over at Katie, her green eyes dark with excitement and cheeks flushed from the wine.

A sharp pang of worry threatened the moment. He'd hit a small snag in his plans and knew he had to tell Katie about Nonna first. It wouldn't be fair to let her say "yes" and then spring it on her. *Please, please, if anybody is up there listening, help a poor guy out!*

"Sweetheart, I had a surprise phone call this week..."

Katie pushed her forehead against the cool bathroom tile and took a deep, shaky breath. *What just happened? It was not supposed to go like this.* The perfect romantic night had turned into a disaster. *How can I go back out there and face him?*

She pulled away from the wall and stared at her reflection in the mirror. Tears glistened in her dark green eyes. One slipped down her cheek and onto the front of her silk jade dress. The dark stain slowly spread like the frustration that crept through her soul.

Dominic Lawrence was perfect. His dark, good looks, and tall, athletic body had women taking a second look whenever he entered the room. They had similar interests but were opposites in personality. He was easy going to her serious nature. She liked to plot and plan; he loved spur-of-the-moment. Her thriftiness made him chuckle. They accepted their differences and balanced one another. And the man could make her blood boil with a look or a touch.

Why now? Fumbling in her purse for her cell, she tried to put things in perspective. *Calm down. He might change his mind. She might not agree.* Katie swiped the screen, her finger slicing across the necks of the happy couple smiling back at her. *That's ironic.*

"Oh my god, you remembered to call me. Did he propose?" her best friend's voice gushed over the line. "Where did he take you?"

"Alinea's." She tried to stamp down the impatience she felt at Jazzy's enthusiasm. "Listen—"

"No way. It's one of the most expensive restaurants in Chicago. He had to buy the tickets months ago." Alinea's, a premiere restaurant on the east side, did not take reservations but sold tickets instead.

"I know. Now listen—"

"I heard they have a green apple helium balloon. It's clear and you put your mouth on it and suck in the flavor. Then the helium affects your voice... Are you crying?"

"No, yes. Oh Jazzy." She let loose a sob as another conversation didn't hit the mark. She felt as if she were in the twilight zone.

"Did he propose?" The excitement was gone from her friend's voice, replaced with concern and wariness.

"Not yet." She held the phone away from ear, anticipating the loud reprimand.

"WHAT? Where are you? The *bathroom*?"

"Yes, but I—"

"It's just a little panic attack. We practiced this. Your traditional Italian man gets down on one knee.

He says something so tender and sweet that you smile, get a little moisture in your eyes—"

"He wants to bring his grandmother back from Italy to live with him."

Silence. A speechless Jazzy would be laughable at any other time. "Help me." She hated the pleading in her tone, hated not being in control of a situation.

"Give me a minute, you caught me off guard."

Katie heard the snap of her fingers on the other end. She only did that when she was stumped. *Oh, god.* "What am I going to do? You know I'm not a demonstrative person."

A snort burst through the phone.

"I'm not like the rest of his family. They are in your face, hugging then fighting then hugging again. I need peace. And privacy. And personal space. What if she's like the New York branch?"

"You don't need space from your hunky Italian." Jazzy chuckled. "The Romano family is loud, affectionate and unfiltered. I adore them. But remember, there are dozens of them. Dominic was raised an only child like his father, who was raised by Antonia. His cousins are all on his mother's side."

"I've never met her but he's talked about her so much. His grandmother is all he has left on his father's side. What if she's a domineering matriarch? I can't even cook." She batted a wisp of hair from her eyes, mindless of the pins that threatened to fall from the loose bun. "Or worse, what if she's a decrepit old woman? I have a terrible bedside manner. Can you see me emptying bed pans or feeding someone?"

Laughter bubbled from the phone. "From the stories Dom has told us, she probably has more energy than you. Antonia sounds very independent and may refuse to come back with him."

Katie hadn't thought of that. Perhaps all this drama was premature. "That's a good point. But Dominic doesn't put his foot down often and when he does, he's impossible to sway. He says he owes his life to that woman."

Jazzy took on her let's-be-reasonable tone. "She came back for her son and daughter-in-law's funeral and stayed two years. According to his cousin, Dom would have walked away from the family business if his grandmother hadn't intervened. He owes her a lot."

The tears stung the back of her eyes again and she silently nodded her head. It was time to give back, and the man she loved would never turn his back on family.

"Do you love him?"

"With all my heart." The voice of reason. What would she do without Jazzy?

"Then you can't tell him no."

"But how can I tell him yes?"

Silence. Then a chuckle. "Okay, Plan B. Here's what we do..."

Dominic stared at the empty chair across from him. The whole evening was a catastrophe. He ran his fingers through his hair, sending the thick waves in uneven spikes.

He had planned this evening for six months. The Alinea staff knew him by name. Every detail checked and rechecked, so he only had to worry about stumbling over his own words. This night her eyes would glisten with emotion and their life together would begin. Dominic had left nothing to chance.

Or so he thought.

Yesterday he received a phone call from his grandmother in Italy. Her younger sister had passed away, and Nonna was now living alone at the age of eighty-eight. Insisting she was healthy and mobile, she had only called to let him know of the funeral arrangements. "I knew you would want to attend, and perhaps you could help me with some of the details," she had said then paused. "*Mi manchi*, Nico."

"I miss you too, Nonna," he had answered with a crack in his voice, feeling like a little boy again.

Now he looked at the vacant spot across from him. When he'd told Katie that he wanted to bring his grandmother back with him, it was as if he'd thrown a cold, wet blanket on their fire. She had sat quietly while he tried to explain, make her understand his need to care for his grandmother himself. Then she nodded, murmured an excuse, and practically ran to the restroom.

I'm an idiot. I should have been subtler, led up to it more. But in the end, it didn't matter what Katie thought. He couldn't let Nonna live alone at her age. She had always been there for him. And regardless of the sacrifice, he would be there for her.

He pulled his cell phone from his pocket, scrolled down, and touched Vince's name. *Deep breath, call the man who always has an answer.*

"Hey, Dom. Well, is it official?" His cousin's voice boomed through the tiny speaker and put a grin on his face. In the background, he could hear the chatter of several women and his uncle competing to be heard.

"There's been a slight hitch."

"He's getting hitched, Ma." A muffled cheer then Vince added, "Ma wants you on speaker phone."

"No, wait. I haven't—"

"Dommi, your mamma would be so happy and your papa so proud," gushed his Aunt Maria. "We need that Skip thing so we can kiss you through the screen. Kathleen is a lucky girl."

"Zia, you don't understand. I haven't asked her yet."

"*Perche no?* What is taking you so long?" She began making shushing noises at his cousins. He could almost see her arm flapping at the three youngest girls, Bianca, Bella, and Gemma.

"Congratulations, Dommi," yelled the twelve-year-old Gemma.

"We love you."

"Give Katie a big hug from us," added the teenage twins, Bianca and Bella.

"Zia Maria, I need to talk to Vince." His fingers clutched the phone and he tried to keep his voice down. He glanced at the closest table but they had gone through several bottles of wine and had their own show going on.

His uncle's voice bellowed over the racket. "Why are you calling us then? Did she stand you up?"

Dominic ran a hand over his eyes. "No, Zio Tony. She's in the bathroom. Now let me talk to Vince."

"You're calling us while she takes a potty break? Vincenzo, take a lesson from your cousin on what *not* to do when you get engaged. In my day, a man..."

He heard a click and the voices faded slightly. "Sorry, Dom. I had to retreat to the roof." The sound of Brooklyn traffic somehow calmed his nerves after the speaker chat with Vincenzo's family. "What's up? It's your big night, bro. That chef has bled you dry with special orders, promising a night to remember."

Lawrence Produce and Supply catered to the high-end restaurants of Chicago. If black truffles were in short supply, his business found them. Vince traveled around the world to wheel, deal, and woo international export traders for the delicacies wanted by Michelin star chefs. Dominic sold them to the highest bidder. Or gave them away to have in exchange for the most memorable night of Katie's life.

"He's living up to his reputation and his promise. That's not the problem." Dom looked nervously at the doorway, not wanting to be caught on the phone. "It's Nonna."

"Nonna's there?"

Air escaped his lungs and his cheeks puffed out as he gave himself a face palm. "No, she called a couple days ago, remember?"

"Of course, how is she doing since her sister died?"

"Fine. But I hear the strain in her voice. I'm going to Italy for the funeral and bringing her back."

"Yeah, we figured as much. So Katie's not so happy, huh?"

"She practically ran for the bathroom. I'm afraid she won't marry me now." There, he'd said it out loud. The elephant in the room was now stomping all over their $1000 meal. "I don't think I can live without her."

"You couldn't live with *yourself* if you didn't help your grandmother."

A quiet pause, then Vince said quietly, "You know we'd be happy to have her here with us. She might like Brooklyn. With just the three girls left, there's plenty of room."

Dominic smiled and nodded his head. "I know you would. But she'll either come with me or stay in Italy. The only two places she has ever called home has been Benevento or Chicago."

"The way I see it, if Katie can't accept that then she's not the girl you thought she was. Better to find out now than later."

Deep down, he knew Vince might be right. But he also hated the timing. If they had been married, and Katie had already grown to love his grandmother, perhaps the look of panic might not have covered her face.

"Yeah, well. Thanks for putting things in perspective. I'd better let you go. She should be back soon." He ended the call and replaced the cell in his jacket pocket. Katie walked toward him, her red-rimmed eyes downcast.

He stood and pulled back her chair, leaning down to place a kiss on her cheek. As he sat down across from her, he reached out to hold her hand. "This is not the conversation I had planned for this evening, but I needed to be honest with you."

"I've never even met her. " She pulled her fingers back from his grip and placed her hands in her lap; her eyes remained down, telling him that she was systematically processing the information. "So, you haven't actually discussed this with your grandmother yet, correct? When do you leave?"

"Monday." In a typical Italian gesture, his hands shot out as he tried to explain, "If you just get to her know her. You'll love her as much as I do."

Out of the corner of his eye, he saw the maitre'd move. *No. Not yet. That wasn't the sign.*

He watched Katie's chest rise and fall with several deep breaths; her eyes finally lifted to hold his gaze.

"Why don't we wait and see what happens, okay? I'm sure we can work this out. She may even turn you down."

He opened his mouth to reply but two waiters appeared at the table and laid down a large cement plate. One dropped a spoonful of creamy chocolate here, lemon and orange there, while the other splashed arcs of colorful sauces and syrups, making it look like a wall of graffiti. As the men completed their artwork, Katie peered closely at the plate.

In the middle of the edible artwork, she whispered the words "Marry Me" aloud. Instead of a look of joy, he saw hesitation. His stomach clenched as he rose from his chair and knelt before her. Holding out a black velvet box with a simple princess-cut diamond ring, he took a deep breath.

"Kathleen James, you are the love of my life. Will you marry me and let me spend the rest of my years making you happy?" A drop of sweat rolled down his back; he steadied his hand. Keep it together. You have a fifty-fifty shot now.

Her eyes glittered as her hand flew to her mouth. For a moment, he thought she would run. Instead, she did something totally out of character.

She leaned down, placed her palms on his cheeks, and kissed him tenderly. His heart pounded at this rare public show of affection. He had his answer. Then her hands covered his and slowly pushed down until the box closed.

A single tear slid down her cheek. "I do love you, Dominic Lawrence. But I need more time before you ask me this again."

All you need is love. But a little chocolate now and then doesn't hurt.

Charles Schultz

CHAPTER TWO

The phone rang and Katie considered not answering it. She wasn't up to playing Twenty Questions without some coffee first. Her feet hit the rug by the bed as she reached for the cordless and pushed the button.

"Well, did he ask you? You never called or texted me." Jasmine's voice sounded too demanding for 8:30 in the morning. "What happened with Plan B?"

She padded into her kitchen, grabbed the empty pot, and filled it with water, cradling the phone on her shoulder. "Yes, he proposed. And yes, I went with Plan B." The coffee grinder halted the conversation for a moment.

"And then? Never mind," she said impatiently. "I'll grab some cinnamon and banana muffins from Mariano's and be there in less than half an hour. Save me some coffee."

The line went dead. She better get dressed and decide exactly how to disclose last night's events to her best friend. Without sounding like a selfish little witch. *Why do I feel guilty for not wanting to start out my married life with another woman in my house? Especially an elderly Italian one.* She knew what those matriarchs could be like—bossy, overprotective. Nothing would be good enough for her grandson and everything Katie did would fall short.

She ran a comb through her hair and ignored the self-reproach in the reflection. After a long sigh, she reasoned with the image. "He couldn't expect me to just say yes after such a shock. It's not unreasonable to ask for some time." The guilt did not recede from the eyes in the bathroom mirror. "I at least need to get to know her first."

The aroma of coffee lured her back to the kitchen. Grabbing the hazelnut creamer from the fridge, she poured in too much and let the sweetness ease her mind. Sugar had always been her extreme comfort food; fortunately, she seldom needed it. Chips and fried foods were easy to pass up but desserts and homemade candies took much more willpower.

How was Dom coping with the morning after? Should she call or give him space? Her heart told her to pick up the phone but her common sense said to leave him alone until she knew what to say. As if responding to her dilemma, Vivaldi's Four Seasons played on her cell phone and Dom's face appeared on her screen. A shaky finger swiped across his sexy grin.

Deep breath! "Hi," she said in a small voice.

"Hello, beautiful."

Her heart stopped. She fought to make a sound but her throat constricted, and tears threatened to spill into her coffee. He misread the silence.

"Look, I know I unloaded a bombshell on you and apologize for that. But last night took over six months to arrange. I really did not have the option to postpone it." A ragged sigh followed. "I have to fly into Naples and assist with the arrangements. We won't be back until next week. Nonna will need some time to say goodbye and decide what to bring with her and what to send on—"

"I do love you." *Where had that come from?*

"You have no idea how happy I am to hear that this morning." The relief added a huskiness to his voice and an ache to her heart. She longed to tell him everything would be fine but couldn't form the words. *Why? Why did he tell me now?* But the faint voice of reason told her better now than after they were married. Then she would have no choice.

"Call me when you arrive so I know you made it safely."

"Will do... Katie?" he asked softly. "Promise to give her a chance? I would have lost the business after my parents died if she hadn't come. She stayed for two years just to keep me on track and keep her small foot on my backside. It was Nonna's idea to bring Vince in to help. I don't know where I'd be without her."

Dang. Another tear slipped down her cheek. *It must be that time of month. I'm overemotional.* "I promise. I'm not giving up on us yet."

The *yet* hung in cyberspace between them. Dom's gruff goodbye told her she'd given him a gut punch. *Did you have to say that?* She reached for the creamer but a sharp buzzing rescued her from another shot of sugar. *Jasmine.*

"Jazzy? Is that you?" she asked unnecessarily, pushing the intercom.

"No, it's Cinderella. Hurry up and let me in. The creepy doorman is staring again."

Katie pushed the button with a laugh, glad at the distraction. Her best friend had a love-hate relationship with Thomas. He would smile at her, she would call him a lecherous old man, and he would respond with a wink. If he didn't smile at her, Jasmine rushed to check her make-up. He must not have flashed a grin because she made it up to the forty-fourth floor in record time and pounded on the door.

"Come in, it's open." She watched the slim blonde rush to the hall mirror for a quick self-inspection. "You look fine. He does it on purpose, you know."

"I don't want to talk about it. He's lucky he's not bad-looking for an older guy or I'd have slapped him by now." Jasmine headed into the kitchen. "So tell me about the romantic night that you endured and I would have thoroughly enjoyed."

"What's that supposed to mean?"

Her friend snorted. "You're a CPA. Accountants are efficient not romantic."

"I'm a tax consultant and there is nothing wrong with being practical."

"Well, I'm a fashion designer who spent two hours last night creating a bombshell, all for naught. Nothing practical about that," she mumbled as she opened a cupboard door, grabbed a plate, and dumped three gigantic muffins from the bag. "Do you need a hug?"

"No, thanks. But a few words of sympathy would be nice."

"I've known you since grade school. You have that heartrending look in your eye that I've only seen after your grandfather died." She gave Katie's back a little rub, held the plate under her nose, and moved to the dining room. "If I give you any sympathy, you'll lose it. So I'll treat you like Thomas while you tell me what happened after you left the bathroom last night.

The aroma of fresh baked goods drew her to the table. Cinnamon assailed her nose as she picked up a muffin and tore it in half with her fingers. "Aaah, this doesn't even need butter."

"And I had them add chocolate fudge drizzle. The hazelnut creamer is out? Uhoh, it's going to be a long self-pity day." Jasmine's eyebrows rose as she gazed out the spotless glass and sighed. "You don't know how lucky you are to have this condo and such a view. Hmm, most of the sailboats have gone already. Winter is coming to the Midwest."

"It was a practical investment *and* a great deal." Katie paused, anticipating the groan. *One, two, three... there it is.*

"Aaagh! Look out there at the white caps and yachts and just enjoy the panorama. Dominic has been good for you, but he still has work to do." She popped a chunk of the warm muffin into her mouth and smiled. "So was it romantic?"

"Yes," she replied, easily keeping up with her friend's change in subject.

"Did he have the staff in on it?"

"Yes."

"I can't take it anymore. Spill it, every detail from the time he picked you up at the front door."

She told her everything. It felt good to recount the evening and get it straight in her mind. Her best friend could also be an objective ear since she was also Dom's biggest fan. He had wisely roped her in as an ally early in the relationship. Katie knew when the story leaned in her favor, or not, from the transparent expressions that ran across Jazzy's face. She interrupted at the mention of eighteen courses.

"Wow, I bet you had to bite your tongue on the price of that," she interrupted at the mention of numerous courses. "No, that would have ruined your whole dining experience."

They groaned at the terrible joke together.

"Sorry," Jazzy said with a shake of her head. "I had an image of you calculating how much the restaurant overcharged for each plate."

Katie pressed her lips together.

"I knew it," she said triumphantly. "Okay, the rest of the story."

By the end, Jazzy had tears in her eyes. Her friend had been right; the sympathy threatened her composure.

"This is like a bad romance movie. My sensible friend finds love with the man of her dreams and a bossy Italian matriarch tries to break them apart," Jazzy sniffed. "So you need to stand firm and hold your ground against her. She'll come to grudgingly respect you, and it will all end happily ever after."

Katie chuckled for the first time that morning. "He called earlier to tell me he was leaving and ask me to give her a chance."

"You're killing me. I feel terrible for both of you." She walked around the table and gave her friend a fierce hug. "Maybe Antonia won't come back with him. From what he told me, she's quite a character."

"It sounded like Dominic had made up his mind." She reached for half of the third muffin, looked down at her hips, and put it back.

"Please, you are five feet six, and a size four. Eat the darn thing."

"What am I going to do?" Katie did as she was told, trying to talk around a mouthful of muffin. "We are the perfect couple on paper. I shouldn't let this get in our way. But the thought of another woman watching over my shoulder, judging me... Or what if she needs care? I'm not the nurse type."

"I think Dominic would help his own grandmother. Besides, she can't be around much longer at eighty-eight."

"Jazzy!"

"Well? I mean, realistically, that's ancient.

"If I agree to marry him, his problems will be my problems. It doesn't matter how long."

"Why don't you wait and see if she *is* a problem?" Jazzy held up her hand. "There is the smallest possibility that might you decide you love her like your own—"

"Don't say it. I love my mother but we butt heads constantly."

"That's because she's the doomsayer. Her glass is always half empty. Look, I'm just saying this is a glitch, a bump in the road. I can't imagine Dominic's grandmother being so bad. Look at him."

"You're right. I need to stop thinking about it and just take it a day at a time."

"Are you worried he won't ask you again? Or worried that he will?" The blonde slapped her own forehead. "Sorry! I'll change the subject."

"Dom has great instincts. He'll know if we're getting along, and if it's the best thing for both of us. All of us," Katie corrected herself and poured them another cup of coffee. "The ball is back in his court now. I won't need to bring it up again." She rubbed the third finger of her left hand, not feeling as confident as her words. Would he ever offer that princess-cut diamond again?

For the rest of the morning, Katie picked up the house and read the Sunday paper. She needed to clear her head, so she headed down to the lake and went for a jog. Gusts of wind coming in off the rolling waves invigorated her skin and gave her energy; the run tired her body and her mind.

After a shower, she settled into the raggedy overstuffed chair that had belonged to her grandfather. Her mother hated the piece of furniture, claiming it didn't fit in with the rest of her décor. Of course it didn't. But each time she sank into the old cushions, she once again felt her grandfather's warm embrace. The opposite of her parents, Grandpa Hank had always been warm, affectionate, and ready with a laugh. Much like Dominic, she thought with surprise. How had she not realized that before?

Overt affection had not been part of her upbringing. It wasn't that her parents didn't care; they just didn't talk about love or show affection. Emotions were a private issue only shown behind closed doors. A nanny had raised her until she turned thirteen. Katie had thrown a temper tantrum at the mention of a boarding school. She finally won the public education battle and met her best friend the next day in math class.

It wasn't until her teens that she slowly built a genuine relationship with her mom. Her father often absent, she began to accompany her mother to some of the local charity events and volunteer activities. Her mother's popularity surprised her. She watched Eleanor use her gracious manner and good looks to charm the most tightfisted businessmen into opening their checkbooks. Her fund-raising abilities were legendary; she gathered the most prominent guests and always met or exceeded the monetary goal.

Her parents had also exposed her to the arts and entertainment provided in Chicago, adding sophistication beyond her years. By the time she turned twenty-one, she could select a rare painting from a collection of copies, identify most classical pieces of music, and distinguish an excellent wine from a mediocre vintage by the time she turned twenty-one. She also knew right from wrong, grey from black and white, and that everyone must give back in some way. Her business education began on her sixteenth birthday with extensive travel that led to internships with foreign finance companies. She would soon be ready to take her place as CEO at James' Financial Services.

But was she ready to share her heart and her bed with a man while another woman took over the kitchen?

Dominic Lawrence checked off all the must-haves on her list. His thriving organic business provided fresh produce to the best restaurants in the city and the suburbs. *Successful, check*. Her parents approved of his background and they held the same values. *Shared ethics, check*. They loved the cultural activities Chicago offered: plays, opera, museums, and festivals. Both were physically active and enjoyed biking and running along the lake, hiking and skiing in the winter. *Compatibility, check*.

His Italian descent gave him the tall, dark good looks she'd always preferred. *Handsome, check*. He was devoted to his family and wanted children but did not insist on having them right away. *Dependable, check*. There would be no issues with in-laws and holidays since his parents had died in a car crash ten years earlier, and he was an only child. Not that it was a plus, but she had heard horror stories from her friends about their monster-in-laws fighting over which side had more time with the grandchildren.

On the other hand, they were complete opposites in so many ways. He loved comedy and action flicks but tolerated her docudramas and incessant reading. She needed to have a plan and envied his flexibility. He believed in being frugal throughout the week but letting loose on vacation. She balanced a checkbook to the penny and weighed the importance of all expenditures. She considered punctuality a virtue, while he considered time an approximation.

In general, they complemented one another. He softened her black and white outlook; she gave some edge to his grey areas. Katie found herself enjoying his unexpected surprises. His love of people drew her into surprising and delightful conversations with perfect strangers. Dominic ticked each box. He wasn't perfect, but his flaws defined him as much as his strengths.

No, she didn't throw her arms around him in a passionate hug each time he walked through the door. No, she didn't gush, "I love you," every time he made her heart skip a beat. But he did make her heart skip a beat, and her body always responded when he wrapped his arms around her in a passionate hug. His huge heart and Italian affection had been overwhelming at first, but she had come a long way in adjusting to it during the past year. Dominic called her "a work in progress."

Tears stung her eyes again. So why did she hesitate? He was worth it, wasn't he? But then the Romanos danced before her eyes and her heart beat faster. How would she react if Antonia wanted to embrace her in one of those big Italian bear hugs? Would she think her cold because she didn't return the warmth that came so easily to his family? This was so much more complicated than his grandmother coming to Chicago, she realized. The craving to belong to a loving family had been hidden away since childhood. Now insecurity raised its ugly head.

"Stop it. You are a successful, intelligent woman. Regardless of what happens, you will survive," she told herself in a stern voice. But the panic in her gut did not recede.

Sunday afternoons were always reserved for activities with Dom or a good book. She had been looking forward to a new author Jazzy had recommended and picked up her e-reader. Flipping through the library, she found Blind Love by Kishan Paul. Three hours later, Katie clicked off the e-reader with a sigh. A blind heroine, who'd have thought that would work?

Dark clouds gathered over the lake and rain spit at the glass, making her smile. Storms had never frightened her as a child. On the contrary, she had always enjoyed Mother Nature's temper tantrums. The steady beat of rain on the windowpane always soothed her. Now, as the rumbling began again, unease slid up her spine. Kati prayed the streak of lightning that split the sky wasn't an omen of what lay beyond her own horizon.

If I know what love is, it is because of you.

Herman Hesse

CHAPTER THREE

*T*he tires hit the runway with a squeal, jarring him from thoughts of his last night with Katie. The plane bounced twice then finished with a smooth landing. Dominic looked out at the sunshine glinting off the wing and hoped they had the same type of ending. This was their bounce but by Christmas everything would be ironed out and the engagement official. He had not told Nonna about the proposal. She wouldn't come home with him if she thought her presence might interfere with his future. He hoped that omission didn't come back to haunt him.

The seatbelt lights went off, allowing passengers to stretch, reach for overhead bags, and shuffle along the aisle toward the exit. He combed his fingers through his hair and heard his belly growl. The food on the flight hadn't appealed to him—not with his grandmother's cooking only a couple hours away. What would she have prepared for him? A smile played about his lips, anticipating the reunion. Then guilt riddled him when he remembered he hadn't seen her in over a year. *I'll remedy that soon enough.*

Once in the rental car, he punched the Audi into third gear and accelerated onto the highway, Mount Vesuvius and Naples in his rearview mirror. A warm breeze hit his face as he let down the windows, reviving him after the long flight. He remembered flying economy with layovers when he was a kid. Never again. Jet lag hit him hard enough as a first class passenger, and he'd need his head clear if Nonna put up any arguments. Yet, he doubted it. Something in her voice told him she was silently asking for his help. He'd detected sadness, a resignation in her manner, that hadn't been there before. It scared him. His foot unconsciously pushed the gas pedal down a little harder.

Mountains loomed before him, the early morning sun casting shadows here and there on the valleys and harvested golden wheat fields. He sped past vineyards, dotted red and black, their vines wrapped around wooden fences; he breathed in the familiar scent of ripe olives, peeping beneath the green and silver leaves of hundred-year-old groves. After an hour of twisting roads through the Apennines, Benevento rose in the distance.

Almost there. I hope she has some fresh biscotti cooling on the table.

Joy pumped through his veins, as it did every time he approached this timeworn city. It had that perfect combination of ancient and modern. The local Saturday market showed off the old-world skills of local artisans and farmers under the shade of progressive industrial offices housed in centuries-old buildings. And there were few tourists. Benevento had grown into the 21st century gracefully and without notice.

He shifted to a lower gear as the car climbed a hill, stopping in front of the little terracotta-colored stone cottage just outside the city limits. It was another mile into the town center, and Antonia Lawrence walked it everyday. Music floated through the window, an old Italian lullaby he recognized from his youth, his grandmother's soft, low voice blending with the melody. The smell of freshly roasted espresso mixed with the sweet scent of Bougainvillea hanging on the windowsills that flanked the front door.

"Ciao, Nonna," he said softly through the window, not wanting to startle her. He spotted a plate of Italian cookies and rubbed his hands together.

"Nico, my Nico." A chair scraped over the tile floor and a swirl of bright green, peach, and gray swept past the window. The door opened and the elderly woman stepped into his arms. Her head barely reached his chest but her slight frame still held strength as she squeezed the breath out of him.

"I have missed you, *il mio dolce nipote*," Antonia said as she reached up with both hands and pulled his head down. After placing a kiss on his forehead, she promptly pinched his cheek. "You told me the plane arrived early morning. I have been waiting for hours, I was worried."

"Nonna, it's only ten o'clock."

"I rise with the sun, half the day is over by mid-morning," she scolded with a wagging finger, a gleam brightening her faded blue eyes. "Come in and sit. I have been busy baking your favorites, and your room is prepared."

Dominic ducked his head as he entered the small doorway and took in the aged furniture and household smells. This was Italy for him. Herbs hung upside down to dry from the oak rafters; the scent of rosemary and basil filled the room along with the sweet aroma of pistachios from the biscotti. Old photographs filled the top of a piano occupying the corner of the room.

His grandmother had grown up in this house. Memories whispered to him from the old stone and plaster walls. The years had smoothed the rough edges into minor bumps, adding character to the structure. Looking at the lined face of his grandmother, he realized time had the opposite effect on people.

His first memory of this place had been with his grandparents. Once they could afford it, Antonia had visited her mother and father at least every other year. When Dominic turned seven, she made it an annual trip and insisted he accompany them so he would know his family "from the boot." Dominic's father had smiled, explaining to his wife that he had done the same as a boy. She had reluctantly agreed with the stipulation that she could accompany them for part of the time. After the first visit, his mother had fallen in love with the countryside.

He loved spending summers with the Capriottis. His great-grandparents didn't dote on him, and didn't talk to him as if he were a little kid. Nonna's sister and several of her grown children, with families of their own, often came to Benevento at the same time. He worked alongside his second cousins, in the fields and helping in *Bisnonno's ristorante*. In the afternoons, they wrestled, played tag, and found whatever trouble they could. A scraped knee could send his mother into hysteria at home but was part of the day's events in Italy. And in the evening, it was all about the food. The family gathered around the table and ate, laughed, and shared their day. As an adult, he missed those happy, carefree days.

Guido and Fedora, in their sixties, had passed within weeks of each other: Fedora of cancer, and Guido of a broken heart. Great Aunt Sophia, recently widowed, then moved into the house. Keeping with tradition, Nonna had also returned home when Grandpa Ken had died.

Dominic wandered over to the piano and perused the old black and white photos. His favorites were those of Nonna, Grandpa, and their collie mix, Dante. His grandparents had met during World War II when Ken Lawrence's air squadron was stationed in Italy. Antonia's family had owned a small café and made a decent living providing liqueur and sticky buns to the American soldiers. Dante, finding a steady handout from the pilot, had befriended Ken on one of his stops at the café. Years later, Nonna still insisted she would never have looked twice at *that gangly American* had it not been for the intuitive collie.

He felt a hand on his shoulder and put his arm around the tiny woman, a melancholy settling over him. Her life was coming to a close and his just beginning. What went through her mind these days?

As if reading his thoughts, she spoke, "I have no regrets, you know. I have had a rich life full of love and happiness. There is nothing I would take back or do over." She patted his arm. "Come, sit, and tell me how you have been."

Dominic eased into one of the old wooden chairs and put his elbows on the worn table as Antonia brewed a small cup of espresso. The machine had been a birthday gift from him and one of the few modern gadgets in the house. Microwaves produced cancer and hands washed a dish better than any machine.

He chuckled when he remembered the argument she'd had with his mother. "Antonia, you need a new washer and dryer," his mother had said, hands on her hips. "You can't continue to use that outdated wringer. It's too hard on your poor old back."

Seeing the look on Nonna's face at the mention of her age, Grandpa had run for cover. His father tried to smooth things over. "Momma, we just want to help—"

"Come ti permetti! There is nothing wrong with my back." Nonna's voice rose along with her indignation.

"How dare I what?" an equally indignant daughter-in-law asked just as loudly. "How dare I worry about you working too hard and wearing yourself out? How dare I be selfish and want you to be healthy and whole for as long as possible because I love you so much?"

Both women had dissolved into tears, hugging each other and apologizing. This signaled the men that it was safe to come back into the room. Antonia had loved his mother as if she'd been her own daughter. She had handpicked " the nice Italian girl" for her son; a fact he remained ignorant of until several years into their marriage.

"Nonna, you look good, and those colors are beautiful on you," he said as he dunked one of the oblong cookies into his coffee. "I'm surprised you aren't in black."

"Sophia hated black. I'll wear mourning clothes tomorrow to the church. The children arrived yesterday and we will see them tomorrow," she said as she pushed the plate toward him. "Eat, *caro*, you look skinny."

A laugh rumbled up from his belly. "You are the only person I know who would call me skinny. I'm sure I'll be a few pounds heavier before we head back home."

"We? Is someone else coming?"

You idiot! "Uh, no. I didn't mean to bring it up this soon but I was hoping you would return with me," he answered with a sheepish grin.

"For how long?" Antonia busied herself with her cup, moving the handle around until it lined up with a crack in the old saucer, fitting it into the indented circle, and running her finger around the rim. "Where would I stay?"

"With me, Nonna, I want you to come back home."

"I can take care of myself. I do not need a nursemaid." Her chin jutted out and he took a deep breath, preparing for the battle.

"That's not the point. You only came back to Italy because *Bisnonno* died, and you wanted to help Aunt Sophia since she was a widow too. But you are alone now—her kids are spread from France to Sweden..." He reached across the table and took her hand. "Your home has been in Chicago since you were eighteen. It's where you belong. I need you—we need each other."

She smiled through the tears in her eyes and pushed her slender fingers through her thick white hair. "Your parents would be proud of you. What a thoughtful, kind man you have become. I shall think on it."

"Fair enough. Now, show me that list so I can see how busy I'll be this next week."

The funeral was held in Santa Sofia, the town's oldest church. Dominic stood in the entrance, his grandmother on his arm, and absorbed the impression of age and reverence. Six white limestone pillars, connected by arches, stood on each side and separated the long center of the church from the side apses. Between the pillars, he caught glimpses of the eighth and ninth century frescoes that had kept him occupied during long masses as a boy. *Hello, old friends.*

They stopped just inside, dipped their fingers into the holy water, and made the sign of the cross. Dominic escorted his grandmother to a front pew, next to Sophia's two daughters and their families, then retreated outside to help carry in the casket. It was an honor to bearer and he took his place next to his second cousin. But his mind was on Nonna. She had looked older this morning, and he knew she hadn't slept well. He only hoped it was due to heartache from the loss of her sister rather than his premature declaration yesterday.

The funeral procession to the gravesite was small compared to many, but those attending were sincere in their condolences. When the priest finished, Sophia's children spoke about her and shared a memory. The group moved forward, one at a time, to throw a handful of dirt onto the coffin and offer words of sympathy as they left the ceremony. Antonia seemed to shrink a little after each soft murmur, and Dominic put an arm around her for support.

When the immediate family was alone, they each placed a single chrysanthemum upon Sophia's casket. The girls gave their *zia* a long, tearful hug; the oldest whispered something in her ear. Nonna seemed almost afraid to let go of her nieces—as if she would let go of her sister when she did. Her nephew put a hand on her shoulder and asked if she needed anything. She gave him a weak smile.

"I thought I was prepared for this. I thought I had said goodbye to my sister. Yet, I find it harder now than when I held her hand and she took her last breath."

"Are you up for the dinner in town? I'm sure everyone would understand if you went home," asked Dominic. He turned to his Sophia's family and they murmured in agreement.

"No. It will be good for me, all the memories and the stories retold." She tilted her head up and patted his cheek, looking around her extended family. "We will enjoy it, you will see. There may be some stories you have not heard."

She was right. The oldest people from the town reminisced about Sophia and her flirtatious ways with the soldiers during the war. But an Englishman stationed in Foggia, a friend of Grandpa Ken, had stolen her heart. She had lived in England for most of their married life but returned often to her beloved home in the hills of Italy.

That night, over a glass of sweet Strega, he got the courage to ask, "What was in the velvet bag that Aunt Sophia held?"

"The pearl necklace your Uncle Eric gave her on their wedding day, her most precious belonging. I wanted her to rest in peace," she explained and made the sign of the cross, "so I buried it with her."

He'd forgotten about the ancient superstition. Many of the older generation did not speak of the dead after the mourning period, afraid it would summon them back to earth. The thought produced a bittersweet smile. If that were true, his parents would have come back long ago.

Nonna had a faraway expression on her face. "What are you thinking about?"

"The day Papa told us we must go back to work at the cafe. The main streets had been cleared of most of the rubble and the Americans occupied the area. We were relieved but also scared to death." She waved her hand in the air. "You don't want to me retell that old story again."

"Ha! Of course I do. The tales of your youth make great bedtime stories for an adult grandson," he teased her and leaned back with eyes closed. "It's been a long time, Nonna. I'd love to hear it again."

"Well, let's see... the Allied Forces had chased out the Germans. We were happy to see them go but paid a price. Over a thousand civilians died during that march and over half the town destroyed, including Benevento Cathedral. Between the American bombers and the German tanks, we considered ourselves lucky there had been anything left standing. Papa sent us to his mother's old house above the town to keep us safe."

Her voice took on a distant tone, as if she replayed the scene in her mind like an old movie to be watched over and over again. "The British had captured Foggia to use any air strips not destroyed by the retreating army. The Yanks, as everyone called the Americans, set up an intelligence base in Naples along the east coast. Benevento lay in the middle... "

October 1943

Sophia pulled on her sister's sleeve. "Hurry, hurry, another one is coming over the mountain." The girls liked to count the number of aircraft that flew across their mountains between Foggia and Naples. They saw mostly British patrols but the American planes had increased over the past week. They ran outside and watched the British patrol plane move toward them, temporarily blocking the sun. Another Tommie.

Antonia grabbed a handful of material as a gust of wind whipped the skirt around her knees and gazed at the whirling propellers and the sun glint off a silver wing. Sophia tried to hold her hair in place as she lifted her face to the sky, as if the pilot would be able to see her waving. Last night, she had insisted on a style like Rita Hayworth, and Antonia had worked through the evening to tame the mass of curls into smooth waves. Now her sister's shoulder length tresses rebelled and swirled against her face.

Her father hinted that they should have been down in the city helping clean up the rubble but his wife had told him to hush. "Guido, let your daughters pretend for one afternoon there is no war, eh? Can you give them a few hours?"

He had tried to convince his wife and eldest daughter that the arrival of American soldiers meant a faster end to the war. Antonia argued soldiers were soldiers, regardless of what uniform they wore. Too many friends and relatives had lost their homes and businesses when armies commandeered the property for military use. What did it matter if it were a German, English, or even Italian captain giving the order? The family was still homeless. The only males she wished to associate with these days were her father and her dog, Dante.

The first view of her beloved Benevento after the September invasion, along with the lists of dead and missing, had been devastating for the mid-sized community. So many friends and family killed, missing or on the road to Naples. She and her sister had climbed the heavy grey stone, once part of the cathedral, looking for anything salvageable in the debris, but piles of smaller rock made it too treacherous. After one small avalanche and a scraped up leg, her mother called them back.

Shards of colored glass, once proudly illuminated by God's light and the sun, now added a multi-hued tint to the heaps of smashed wood, cement, and wreckage. The shop fronts that managed to stay erect glared at them through gaping holes in the jagged windows. Fedora had sunk to her knees and covered her face as she silently cried. The girls had rushed to their mother's side but had no words of comfort that day. Their father, as always, pulled a shred of hope from the ruins.

"Our café is not gone. We can board up the window. The display is cracked but useable. We will survive this."

A month later, his family was forced to agree. Guido, always the businessman, had insisted his family learn English before the war in order to converse with any tourists that might pass through from Naples. Their command of the language now enabled them to barter and sell baked goods and other supplies he mysteriously found on his "trips." They did not make a fortune but enough to feed themselves and keep a roof over their head.

The remaining citizens worked together with the Yanks to clear the main street enough so wagons, carts, and vehicles could get through—if the mud was not too bad. Their father, well respected in the community along with having the ability to translate, became a vital member of the clean up project. His new foreign connections also brought in news as well as business.

"The Americans are running supplies between Naples and Foggia now. I think we should add some sticky buns to the menu." Guido rubbed his hands together, the anticipation of added income gleaming in his black eyes. "The Yanks will pay good lire for something that reminds them of home."

"Sticky buns?" Antonia asked. "Now what are you getting Mamma into?"

""*An Americano came in and told me about them. It's sweet roll, that's all, but we line the bottom of the pan with honey and nuts. When you flip the bread out, the bottom becomes the topping.*" Guido's thumb touched each finger, indicating he silently calculated the numbers in his head. "*I told him if he brings me some good yeast, we will make them unique by adding our local liqueur.*"

"*Are we to go back to work at the café then?*" Antonia felt a wet tongue on her hand and buried her fingers in Dante's soft fur. Her father insisted the dog was not a mongrel, but the old priest at Santa Sophia contended that a true collie had a longer nose. "*Dante does not like soldiers. He will growl as soon as one walks through the door.*"

"*Yes, cara. It is safe enough in the town during the day. Your mother and I need your help or we will all starve.*" He wagged a finger at the sable and white dog. "*How does the animal manage to stay cleaner than I do? Lock him in the backroom during the day if he barks too much. He will be good protection when you walk to and from the town. I don't think we should move back into town yet.*"

"Nico, you must do me a favor." Antonia's eyes focused again, and she shifted in her chair before the fire. The shadows from the flames made her look years younger, and he saw traces of the beautiful young woman who met her only love seventy years earlier. "I want to be buried with our photograph."

He didn't need to ask. "The one with you and Grandpa and Dante."

"Yes, *caro*," she said is a soft voice, "that one."

"I promise, Nonna." He reached over and grasped her hand but refrained from squeezing it with all the emotion he felt. "That won't be for a long time, though."

"No, no it won't." She said in a forced, cheery tone. "So you are sure you have room for me?"

After his last rejection, he refused to get his hopes up. "You know I'm still in Mom and Dad's house. There's your old room on the second floor with your own bath, or I could move my office to the top level so you can avoid the stairs. You'd have complete control of the kitchen."

She chuckled. "Of course I would. And your lady in Chicago, Katie... She would not disapprove of an old woman living in your house? You have no immediate plans?"

He hesitated but said truthfully, "None, and she'll love you as I do."

"*Va bene.* It is time to go home. I want to end my life where it truly began—with your grandfather. "

Dominic realized his intuition had been right; she was lonely and homesick. He got up from the chair and knelt in front of her, taking her slender fingers gently in his. "We won't sell this house. If you aren't happy, I will bring you back to Benevento and figure something out. I am so happy to bring you home with me."

She gently withdrew her hands, placed them on either side of his face, and looked at him intently before speaking, "The words sound sincere but the sadness in your eyes tells a different story. I believe there is more going on in your life than what you say." She kissed his forehead. "But trust me, Nico, I will find it all out."

He had no doubt she would, and it scared the hell out of him. Maybe he'd light an extra candle at Santa Sofia for himself before they left. If the two women he loved the most in the world combined forces against him, nothing short of divine intervention could save him.

*When you trip over love, it is easy to get up.
But when you fall in love, it is impossible to
stand again.*

Albert Einstein

CHAPTER FOUR

The glowing red numbers on the clock radio clicked to 5:00 a.m. as the pillow flew across the room and hit the bedroom wall with a *whoomf*! Katie tossed the blankets back with a growl. *Might as well get up, you've been tossing and turning since three.* Her feet hit the floor, toes wriggling into her slippers. She jerked her robe off the bedpost and headed for the kitchen.

At least she had plenty of time to prepare for her weekly Friday board meeting. Hitting the switch on the coffee maker, the aroma of fresh Colombian wafted up to her nose and settled her mood. It had been almost a week since Dom left for Italy. He'd called twice; the second time to let her know he would be there longer than expected. Antonia *would* be coming home with him.

When he asked her to meet them at the airport the following Thursday, she hesitated. "Don't worry about it," he'd said after the pause. "I'll hire a service, I know you're working and busy."

"No, I can do it. Really, I don't mind." Even to her ears, the words sounded forced.

"Look, I'll call you when we get settled in and you can come over for dinner." In a hopeful tone, he added, "Nonna is a great cook, and she'll whip you up one of her specialties."

Stifling the groan at the cooking comment, she wondered if Dom had informed her that his fiancée—no, girlfriend—was an idiot in the kitchen. In fact, Katie wondered exactly what he *had* told his grandmother about the whole situation. In one more week, she could ask him in person.

One more week with this knot in her stomach. The realization of how dependent she had become on Dom's companionship startled her. She took for granted the quick phone calls or texts to tell him about her day or the pictures she passed on when she came across something unusual. Sometimes it was just a funny sticker sent to let him know her mood. Until now, she hadn't noticed what an integral part he played in her daily routine. With the recent events and emotions welling up inside her, Katie now found herself hesitant to even text. God, she missed him. Adding to the loneliness was guilt. It had become her constant companion in his absence.

The board meeting ended and Katie smiled, happy with the outcome. She had recommended the buyout of two smaller public companies. Her research had shown that profits would increase within the first three years, and eventually, add five to seven percent in the value of their own company's stock. The youngest member of the board was twenty years her senior but they had listened intently and agreed with her findings. James Financial Services did not worry about instant capital. They looked at the big picture and could afford to sit on a nest egg and wait for it to grow.

Her father beamed with pride when the vice-president commented on her intuitive business mind and impressive track record in the five years she had joined the company. Still, she cringed when she heard the "chip off the old block" from one of the senior partners.

As the room cleared out, her father motioned her to stay. "Nice work, Kathleen. I'm proud of you." He gave her a pat on the back. "Stop by my office. I need to talk to you about something."

Assuming he wanted to discuss more details on the buyout, she was surprised to see her mother sitting in front of the large walnut desk. "Hello dear," Eleanor said and gave a quick half-kiss to each cheek. "I heard you impressed the board once again."

Katie nodded and smiled. A job well done, and well presented, always gave her a sense of satisfaction. There was nothing like that feeling when all the numbers fell into place.

Then it hit her. Her parents wanted to know about her night with Dominic. It was no surprise they hadn't called. The Lawrences believed in giving their daughter "her space."

Sinking down into the chair next to her mother, she asked, "What brings you into the city in the middle of the day?"

"Just some errands."

Her father pulled at his tie and looked uncomfortable. "We were wondering what happened the other night on your date with Dominic?"

Oh god, I don't think I can do this. Rather than lie, she told a partial truth. "His great aunt died and he had to fly to Italy to help his grandmother with the arrangements. He won't be back until next week," she explained in a tone she hoped sounded normal. The explanation would buy her a little time.

"I'm sorry to hear that," her mother said with the appropriate amount of sympathy in her tone. "Well, we'll be anxious to know when your date is rescheduled. There are so many plans to make—"

"Eleanor, perhaps you should wait until it's official," her father said. "No use taking out the checkbook until there's a ring."

Her parents wanted her to be happy but also wanted her to marry someone of equal social status. Dominic fit the bill. Lawrence Organic Produce continued to expand. Dad thought "the boy" had good business sense and, as her mother had said, "You two will make such pretty babies."

"So," she asked, desperate to change the subject, "are you and Dad going out to lunch? I'm meeting Jazzy at Heaven On Seven if you'd like to join us."

"Why that sounds lovely but your father and I have plans this afternoon, don't we dear?"

"Er, yes..." Her father's voice trailed off and he shot a quick sideways glance at his wife. " "I, uh—"

"She doesn't know yet? Oh dear lord. You promised two weeks ago, Franklin." Her mother crossed her arms and went into a classic scolding mode. "We have plans for a European tour as soon as your father announces his retirement. Your father was supposed to tell you."

"So you decided on a date?"

"That was what we wanted to talk to you about," her mother said in that brace-yourself-and-be-a-big-girl tone. "He's retiring the first of the year. We would like you to stand by your father when he addresses the staff."

"Of course. And what will he be announcing, exactly?" A two-ton brick had just landed on her shoulders. He was sixty-three; they had discussed his upcoming retirement at length, as a family, without committing to an exact day.

She had thought herself prepared but the reality of it put lead in her feet. Would he expect her to take over? What if she wasn't ready?

"Get the look of panic off your face, Kathleen." Her father came up beside her and gave her shoulder a rare squeeze. "I'm relinquishing the throne to our VP, one of the options we've considered together. I won't throw you to the wolves until you are comfortable running the business. I'm only a phone call away, and you'll have the board members to advise you."

"When will you release your statement?" Katie knew it had to be soon. This was October. Her head spun; less than three months to make a smooth transition. "Will you remain on the board?"

"Of course," he barked, then lowered his voice. "I've spent forty-two years of my life building this corporation. I'm not about to walk away."

"I've put a few years into it myself," she said, disliking the pouty tone in her own voice. What was wrong with her? First, she panics that she may have to take over and then she gets sulky that she isn't? "I still thought I might be considered as CEO. Isn't that what you've trained me for?"

Her mother cut in quickly, reaching over to pat her hand. "You can blame that on me. I won't allow my daughter to follow her father's example. You'll soon embark on a new journey with Dominic and need time to build a life together." She looked pointedly at Franklin. "Think back on how often you saw your father when you were a child. I know it was necessary at the time, but you don't need to make the same mistakes we did."

Franklin put an arm around his wife and smiled with genuine affection. "She has been an angel through the years, keeping the ship afloat while I practically lived at the office. I think I owe her some quality time."

Katie tried not to let her mouth fall into her lap as she watched her parents. Hell must be freezing over; her father looked at her mother with stars in his eyes. "Are you dying? Is it cancer?"

They both laughed. "No sweetheart. We hit a certain age, woke up one morning, and realized that life is too short. Our bucket list has been forty years in the making, and it will take another twenty to cross everything off." He chuckled. "We need to grab that golden ring before arthritis takes over, and we can't raise our arms above our heads."

And when did either of you acquire a sense of humor?

"After Christmas, we are taking a six-month cruise. We'll begin the life of leisure he has promised me for the past five years..." Eleanor's eyes pinned on her husband before continuing in a sweet voice, "or I go without him.

Katie smiled. She liked this new side to her parents. Maybe there was hope for her. If an old dog...

The future now seemed brighter. Granted, her father's retirement and the transition period would take away time from Dominic, but it was temporary. He ran his own business and would understand. Plus, it would help keep her mind off meeting Antonia. The heaviness in her chest eased.

The hostess escorted her to a table by the window, and she sank into the chair. Coffee, she needed some caffeine to get her through the rest of the day. Heaven on Seven, her favorite place for lunch, served some of the best Cajun food in the city. If this didn't stir her appetite, nothing would.

Located on the seventh floor, the restaurant overlooked Wabash Avenue. She looked at the crowded street below and wanted to melt into the crowd and lose herself in the anonymity. Her brain almost hurt from so much introspection over the past few days.

"You look like crap." Jazzy came up behind her, put a finger under her chin, and studied her face. "When was the last time you slept through the night?"

Katie opened her mouth then thought the better of it, responding with a shrug. Jazzy's blonde hair, shining in the sunlight that slanted through the window, gave her an angelic appearance. But the low-cut, turquoise top and tight-fitting jeans said otherwise. Why hadn't she been blessed with curves like that?

"I'd say it's been since just before the proposal fiasco."

"I know. And I'm almost ready to slurp down some of that awful green cold medicine just to get a good night's sleep." She could hear the exhaustion in her voice and knew it hadn't escaped her friend—or her parents.

"Have you heard from him?"

"Not since he told me when he and his grandmother would arrive." The knot tightened in her stomach. "Can I tell you how much I don't like myself right now? What is wrong with me, worried about a little old lady?"

Jazzy reached out and squeezed her hand. "He just took you by surprise, that's all. If I were you, I'd call him Thursday night, tell him you missed him, and how much you're looking forward to meeting her."

She nodded but couldn't speak, a lump forming in her throat.

"Would you like me to come with you for the first meeting?"

Katie managed a weak smile. "To hold my hand?"

"I don't think Dominic would care if it got the three of you together. It might make it less stressful and more like a welcoming party," she said as the waitress approached the table. "But it should be your idea."

"I think that might work." Her stomach unclenched just a tad then growled. "Thanks, Jazzy. I don't know what I'd do without you."

"You would have a non-existent love life, never coordinate your outfits and accessories, and wish you had a friend just like me. Now order something loaded with calories that screams comfort food."

The waitress chuckled, ready with her pen. "It sounds like you need the Cajun fried chicken salad and jalapeno corn muffin, honey."

Katie laughed for the first time since the weekend. "Yes, that sounds perfect." She felt Jasmine kick her under the table. Looking up, she spotted Dominic's cousin Vince heading toward her table. *What did I do in a former life to deserve this past week?*

"Hello, Katie," the gorgeous Italian said with an exaggerated bow. "Jasmine," his voice deepening as he reached for her hand and kissed it. "How have you been?"

"The fashion business is booming, Mr. Romano. We just pulled in another big department store." She laughed and shrugged her shoulders. "Not exactly the red carpet designer's dream I had during college, but it's job security."

"Your time will come. My father says hard work and talent will always prevail." He turned his dark eyes on Katie and she mentally squirmed. "How goes it with my cousin Dom?"

"You haven't talked to him?" She cast a frantic look across the table. *Help!*

Jazzy caught the cue and ran with it. "Jeez, you know Antonia's sister died. He had to rush to Italy to help his grandmother with the arrangements. He won't be back until some time next week."

"So, are you joining the family?" he asked Katie without taking his gaze off Jazzy.

She thought of the sparkling rock sitting in a black velvet box and bit her tongue. "We are discussing it when Dom gets back." She closed her eyes in silent thanks as the waitress returned, excused herself, and sidled between the six-foot-plus Italian and the table with her tray. With an appreciative smile at the man next to her, the older woman set down two cups of soup and a plate of muffins.

"That gumbo is especially good today," he informed no one in particular as he sniffed at the cup of soup passing in front of him. He put a hand on the back of Jazzy's chair and the other on the table, leaning in close. "I hope you like spicy."

There was a chorus of groans and eye rolls from the girls. He chuckled. "A little to thick?"

"Just a tad," she agreed, patting his arm. Vince always hit up on her friend when he came into town. He had confided to his cousin that she was on *his* bucket list.

"So what delicacies have you purchased for Lawrence Organic?"

"I just got back from Périgord, France with some duck liver—"

Jazzy spit out her soup.

Vince never blinked. He picked up the napkin from the blonde's lap, the spray from his crotch as he maintained eye contact, then dabbed her chin with it. "As I was saying, I managed a new import contract with an established French company for foie gras and black truffles."

She and Dom had shared the Black Truffle Explosion last weekend. "At Alinea's we had..."

His dark eyes were suddenly on her, boring into her like a drill searching for oil. "I know," he replied a shortly, informing her that he knew plenty about that night.

She fidgeted with the napkin in her lap and kept her eyes cast to the floor. Why did she bring that up? And what did the rest of the family think of her? Did they all know? As if reading her mind, Vince answered her questions is a softer tone.

"Look Katie, we all love you. And we get that this is a unique and difficult situation. But we also hope that you trust your instincts and give Antonia a chance. She's not... Well, let's just say she has a different style from us Romanos. In case you were wondering." He shrugged. "I saw the look of terror on your face the last time all three of my sisters charged you at the door. It's just our way. But you'll find his nonna a bit more, um, refined."

The familiar sting of tears again. So, they had figured her out but still liked her. Her face reddened with shame at the unkind thoughts she'd had of his family. She picked at her food to avoid looking up.

"But more than anything, we want what is best for our Nico," he added firmly, placing a hand on her shoulder. "So if you can't be the wife he needs and accept his offer with no regrets, don't lead him on. He's had enough disappointment in his life."

The bite of muffin stuck in her throat. How could she tell him, even if she wanted to help with Antonia, that her personal time would be limited for the next few months? They would barely have any time for the two of them, let alone a third wheel. So instead, she just nodded.

"Well, I'll leave you girls to your lunch. Your soup is getting cold." He winked at Jazzy and walked away with an exaggerated swagger.

"I bet that man is good." She pulled her blonde hair off her neck and fanned herself with the other hand. "Look at how he fills out those clothes."

"Yeah, a real Romeo."

She drained the iced tea to erase the burning in her chest. But it wasn't the jalapeno that caused her heart to ache.

"There's no substitute for a great love who says, 'No matter what's wrong with you, you're welcome at this table'."

Tom Hanks

CHAPTER FIVE

*D*ominic stared at his cell phone, his finger hovering over the send button. He couldn't decide whether to call or text. If he called, he might hear a tone in her voice that would knock him in the gut. If he texted, she could gracefully back out of the visit.

"Nico, what is wrong? Just talk to the girl." Nonna busied herself in the kitchen, mixing flour and water for gnocchi. "I need to know how much to make."

"I was... I was just thinking. Maybe I shouldn't call her on such short notice."

"And yesterday you said we needed rest after the long flight. Didn't you tell her when we would be back?" Antonia rinsed off her hands and wiped them on the apron she wore over her knee-length cotton dress. "I am asking you again, Nico. What are you worried about?"

He sighed, realizing how hard it would be to hide anything from this intuitive old woman. "Okay. I don't know what I would do if the gals I loved most in my life did not at least like each other." There, he'd said it, and the ache in his heart lessened a bit.

Antonia hurried into the room. "Bend down here, Nico. You are too tall for me to keep stretching on my tiptoes."

He did as he ordered and felt her cold hands on his cheeks; the smell of fresh dough filled his senses. His stomach growled and they both smiled.

"You never told me you loved her. That makes all the difference." She gave him a kiss on each cheek. "I can't imagine you falling for someone who was not a good person. I have seen her pictures. If she is as pretty inside as outside, we will get along fine."

She let him go with a little upward push, turned on her thick square heels, and headed back to the kitchen. "Now call her, *immediato*. Or I will!"

Dominic stared at the back of the light blue and green flowered dress. She sounded just like the grandmother who had ordered him around as a child. *God, I love that woman.*

"What are you laughing at?"

"Nothing, Nonna. I'm going to my room for this phone call so you don't tell me how to make love to her over the phone."

"Don't be smart! What kind of sauce do you want?" she asked over her shoulder." White or red?"

"Red. Everything you need should be in the frig. But no mushrooms, Katie doesn't like them." He closed the door to block out the exclamation he knew would follow. *Buon dio! Who does not like mushrooms?*

Relief swept over him as her voicemail picked up. "Hi, honey. I'm back and Nonna is making cheese

gnocchi tonight. We thought you might like to join us."
He hesitated, then covered his eyes with his hands as
heard his own voice. He continued with more force,
"Listen, if it's too soon, I understand. But call me back
and let me know one way or another. She's really
looking forward to meeting you."

He hit the *end* button and tapped the phone on
his chin. Ten o'clock in the morning. Hopefully, she'd
be on her midday break. Fridays were hectic for her
but she always took a lunch. James' policy demanded
every employee, even the CEO, take a break during the
day. Franklin said it kept the staff fresh and avoided
short-term burnout.

He spent the rest of the morning at his
warehouse, going over imports and returning a week's
worth of messages. His secretary took care of the
routine calls but some clients would only speak with
him. That personal relationship had made him a
successful entrepreneur. He and his cousin personally
brought in all new accounts and maintained
communication with all of their customers at least
monthly. It used to be weekly, but as his business
grew, it became impossible.

Shelley popped her head inside the office. "Katie
is on line 2."

"Got it. Oh, and thank you for holding down the
fort while I was gone. Sorry Vince had to go to France.
I owe you."

"No worries," she said with a smile. "He popped
in last week and checked on things when he got back.
It's always a pleasure to see him." Her eyebrows
wiggled before she shut the door.

Vincenzo managed the international end of
Lawrence Organic Produce. His easy-going but
shrewd nature made him a natural for haggling the

best price on items that couldn't be grown in the States. Fresh truffles from France and Italy were always in demand by high-end restaurants and bringing back top wines had added another profitable venue.

Vince's father was his mom's baby brother. The Romanos and their extended relations made up a small army in New York. The family had their roots in the deep Bronx but now most of them lived in upscale Riverdale, running a produce business that catered to national grocery chains. They were a true Italian family and Dominic had loved visiting the chaotic, loud relatives.

His parents had met when his father had decided to turn Antonia's garden into a business. The Romanos had mutual friends near Naples and had invited the Lawrences to New York for a tour of their own operations. His grandmother had looked over the Romano girls and immediately chosen one for her son. As luck would have it, he had chosen the same one. Family get-togethers were common and the cousins became a tight-knit group.

The two boys, only a year apart, had taken turns staying with each other over summer and holiday vacations and remained close as adults. While he had enjoyed the sense of belonging, the fighting and teasing of the animated siblings, Vince also enjoyed the moments of solitude and attention of a small family. When Dominic found himself running the company alone, his cousin had stepped up to help. They had become partners and the company's profits had doubled.

He picked up the phone and forced his voice to sound cheerful. "Hi, beautiful. What's up?"

"Hello, handsome. Sorry I missed your call." Her voice did a slow burn up his stomach. "The Friday board meeting and all."

Awkward pause. Here it comes...

"Say, would you mind if Jazzy came along for dinner tonight? I thought we'd turn the evening into kind of a welcome party."

"*Yes!* I mean, of course she's welcome. I'll give Nonna a heads-up to set an extra place. Jazz will turn it into quite a celebra—Dammit!"

"What's wrong?"

"It's her birthday. Today is her birthday," he moaned as he gave himself a head slap.

"Don't panic. I'll pick up a gift card at the bookstore and some balloons. You get flowers on your way home. I assume you remember what she likes?"

"Yes, calla lilies," he answered. "Katie?"

"Yes?"

"Thanks. I owe you."

He recognized the sigh on the other end, hurried but pleased. "Just finish up and the get the heck out of there. Don't be late, that's the payback."

"Yes, ma'am. I'm on it."

Dominic finished his last pile of paperwork and headed home to Lincoln Park. He loved the drive up Lake Shore; the traffic rarely bothered him. It was quicker to take public transportation but some days he needed to feel some open space. The view of the water and lack of cement and metal on one side of the highway relieved the cramped and claustrophobic feeling he sometimes got in the city.

He had promised he would only be gone a couple of hours, and it was already two o'clock. He hit the gas and maneuvered the Lexus through the congestion.

Pulling into the garage behind his brick row house, he reached across the seat and grabbed the items Nonna had requested.

"Nico, did you remember the dark chocolate and almonds?" his grandmother asked before he had closed the door behind him.

He strolled into the kitchen and dangled the bag above her head. She smiled and continued stirring a pot of a creamy liquid bubbling on the stove. A delicate, sweetness tickled his nose. "You are *not* making Torta Caprese?"

"It's one of your favorites, and you said Katie likes chocolate."

He rubbed his hands together and licked his lips in anticipation.

She reached up to pinch his chin, and he noticed her flushed cheeks. "Are you feeling okay? Is it too warm in here?"

"I am fine—*splendido*! It feels so good to cook for young ones again." She smoothed her silver hair back with one hand and slapped his fingers with the other as they crept toward the gooey mixture.

"I'm not—

"At my age, you are a youngster. What's behind your back?"

"*Buon compleanno!*" he sang, pulling out the deep orange calla lilies with a flourish.

"You did not forget! Such a sweet boy," she said with a dramatic sigh. "Get a vase, they will be our centerpiece."

He got out his mother's Italian glass vase.

"I remember when Olivia bought that in Venice. She was so worried it would break on the way home," his grandmother reminisced while arranging the flowers in the container. "By the way, is *she* coming?" Her pointed look told him exactly whom she meant.

"Yes, and bringing her best friend Jazzy. Do you mind one more? They want to make it a celebration." He had seen through the ruse; Katie wanted moral support for the introduction. It didn't matter to him how she reached out as long as she did. But he had made a decision today.

There would be no more asking or placating Kathleen James to come on board. This was not a business deal with room for compromise. If she loved him enough, it would work out. He hoped like hell that she would make a life with him and Nonna—but if not, he would move on. He'd rather break his own heart than his grandmother's.

"Jazzy? What kind of a name is that? She sounds like a flapper from the twenties." Antonia shook her head and laughed. "Then it should be a good party. Get out a bottle of Chianti and go change."

"Yes, ma'am. And they'll be here around five."

At exactly five o'clock, the buzzer rang. When he answered the door, Katie's head was turned, saying something to Jazz that made her laugh. His breath hitched at the first glimpse of her in two weeks. The pounding of his heart echoed in his head, desire roared through him. Her effect on him never wavered.

"Welcome to the bash," he said, trying to keep things casual as he stepped aside and dodged the bouquet of floating silver. Katie's eyes locked with his and blushed. "It's good to see you."

"It's good to see to you, too," She moved to her tiptoes and planted a light kiss on his lips.

Before her heels hit the floor, his hands pressed against her hips and pushed her back up. His mouth covered hers, gentle but demanding. He released her slowly, not caring if they had an audience. "That's better."

"It certainly is," she agreed a little breathless.

"Wow, you two should separate more often," Jasmine said in a conspiratorial voice. "You even got me hot."

He leaned down and gave the blonde a peck on the cheek. "I don't want you to feel left out."

The scent of garlic, basil, and oregano drifted into the hall. "Oh my. I'll leave you two alone out here. I must follow my nose."

"We're good for now," Dominic said with a wink at Katie. "It's time for introductions."

Inside he took their jackets and hung them in the hall closet. Her stomach clenched as she waited for her first sight of the woman who had caused so many sleepless nights.

"Nonna, come meet the girls," Dom called from the living room. Out of the kitchen came a tiny woman, barely five feet tall, with shining, silver hair pulled into a perfect chignon. Her features were fine— a straight nose, high cheekbones and wide mouth— and hinted at the beauty she must have been at one time. The blue eyes, so like Dom's, gleamed with a smile, and her olive skin was surprisingly smooth for her age.

"*Ciao*! You must be Katie. You are lovelier than your photographs. *Molto bella donna*," she said with her arms open. "I am so happy to meet you."

Leaning down slightly, she allowed the elderly woman to give her the traditional kiss on both cheeks. "And this is my friend Jasmine."

"You don't look like a flapper but I still think we shall have a good party." Antonia kissed Jazzy too then clapped her hands together. "What's all this?"

The girls held out the half dozen helium balloons decorated with colorful print and flowers, and an envelope. "Happy birthday," they said in unison.

"Nico, you told them? Ah well, get the glasses. We'll start with wine."

Nico? She calls him Nico? A spiral of jealousy sidled through her belly at the thought of someone knowing Dom better than she did. *Stop it! This is his grandmother, for Pete's sake.*

The small group sat down on the worn leather furniture that only a bachelor, or a group of sports fans, could appreciate. The huge sectional had hosted dozens of Sunday night football and hockey games. The three ladies seemed swallowed up by the large furniture while the single male appeared relaxed and at ease.

This is Dom's territory: strong and steady, no frills and immoveable at times. The entire house reflected his personality. She could almost hear his booming voice bouncing off the walls as a football went over the goalpost or the puck missed the net. The old oak woodwork, carved windowsills and crown molding added character to what could have been a slightly shabby interior. He was so different from her father and wondered if that had been part of the attraction. While her father was at the country club rubbing elbows with clients, her boyfriend played tag football at the park.

"So are you all settled in?" she asked, cringing at the stilted, overly polite tone. The Italian woman caught her gaze and held it for a moment. A little unnerved, she looked down at the faded plank floor.

"No, no. I only brought a few things with me on the plane. Nico helped me pack the rest and they should arrive before Thanksgiving. But I want to know more about both of you."

Dom's grandmother intrigued Katie and she soon forgot her nerves. Within minutes, she had both girls feeling welcome and comfortable. She asked countless questions and before dinner knew their jobs, family backgrounds and favorite foods. *He is so much like her in looks and personality. It's no wonder they are close.*

"Come, let's sit at the table." Antonia rose slowly and waved toward the table. "It smells…" She put her fingers to her mouth, kissed them and spread them out, then said in a heavy accent, "Perfetto!"

Jazzy whispered in her ear, "I adore her accent. She sounds like Sophia Loren in those old movies."

"Sophia was a bad girl," Antonia said as she walked to the kitchen. "Much scandal she caused back in Italy."

"What? The movie star?"

"*Si*, the director she fell in love with? Married." She made a *tsk, tsk* noise and wagged her finger. "After his divorce, they did not come back to the homeland for many years. Most Italians are Catholic and never go against their religion or the pope."

"But you didn't marry a Catholic. Did your family approve?" Katie asked. *This is interesting.*

"I had to promise to bring our children up in the church and promptly moved to America." She cupped her hand around one side of her mouth and whispered loudly, "Sophia Loren and I have more in common than you might think."

Jazzy let out a hoot and winked back at Antonia. "Let me help you in the kitchen. We bad girls need to stick together."

"Wait," Katie called after them. "It's your birthday, you shouldn't be cooking. We should take you out."

"In Italy, when we ask friends to celebrate with us, it is our treat. So tonight, I cook!"

Dom grinned from ear to ear and shrugged his shoulders. "That's my Nonna. What do you think?"

"She's adorable. Have you told her I'm dangerous in the kitchen?"

"It doesn't matter. Either you'll take lessons from her or she'll order you out." He moved in front of her and put his arms around her waist, pulling her close. "Seriously, I'm worried about her. Some of the spark is gone, the light that always made everyone smile when she walked into a room."

"It seemed pretty bright to me."

"Tonight, yes. My grandmother loves to entertain. I hope the joy doesn't fade after you girls leave," he said, putting his forehead against hers. "I missed you."

"I missed you too, Dom. I'm sorry I was such a witch before you left," she said softly. "I do want to get to know your grandmother. She seems fascinating."

"You have no idea."

Dinner was spectacular. Thick round slices of mozzarella and tomatoes, sprinkled with olive oil and basil, preceded the main course. The seasoning sat on Katie's tongue and the cheese seemed to melt as she took a sip of wine. Jazzy forgot all table manners as she moaned through gnocchi with ricotta and

Parmesan cheeses, sopping up every drop of the sauce with garlic bread.

While the conversation turned to the coming holidays, Antonia poured each of them a small glass of a yellow liquid. "Nico, get the cake."

Jasmine's eyes widened and her hands went to her belly. "Cake?"

Dom yelled from the kitchen, "Torta Caprese. A little bird told Nonna that someone likes chocolate." He set down a round cake, so dark it was almost black, with powdered sugar sprinkled on the top.

After they each had a slice in front of them, Antonia raised her glass. "To my dearest grandson and my new friends. *Salute!*"

"*Salute,*" they all chanted together.

"Oh my," Jazzy said and licked her lips. "What is this stuff?"

"Strega. It originated in my hometown of Benevento and is used as a... What do you call it? An after-dinner drink. Right, Nico?"

"Yes. It's made out of over seventy herbs and not for the weak-hearted. Don't ask me how I know." He took a bite of cake. "And we use it in desserts."

"It is what brought our family out of poverty during the war," Antonia added. "The American soldiers loved sticky buns. Papa decided to make them with the Strega. Those Yanks paid good money for a sweet that reminded them of home—only better."

"So you made a profit off the war?" Jazzy's eyes narrowed as she looked at the old woman. "I can appreciate that kind of ingenuity."

Katie put the fork to her mouth and closed her eyes. She could smell the richness of the dessert. As the taste of cocoa, almonds, and a hint of mint and juniper from the alcohol hit her tongue, she sounded like Jazzy.

Looking at Antonia, she said in awe, "I think you just became my new best friend."

"I think your grandmother cast a spell on your girlfriend," Jasmine said with a laugh.

"No, I'm afraid I can't take the credit. It is the drink," Antonia pointed to her glass. "The town of Benevento was known as the gathering place for witches. Strega means "witch' in Italian. And it has been known to make people do things they may regret in the morning."

She looked at her grandson and deepened her voice to imitate him, "Don't ask me how I know."

Witchcraft? Maybe there was something to that. Katie had expected this evening to be brutal, hoping to escape as soon as possible. Instead, she had enjoyed the meal, and been charmed by the conversation and company. Perhaps Antonia had brought a bit of Italian enchantment with her.

There is never a time or place for true love. It happens accidentally, in a heartbeat, in a single flashing, throbbing moment.

Sarah Dessen

CHAPTER SIX

The boxes arrived yesterday. Are you still okay with helping Nonna?"

Why had she agreed to this? *You drank too much of that yummy alcohol and would have agreed to almost anything that night.* "Will you be there?"

"Yeees, but don't tell me you are afraid to be alone with my grandmother?" He chuckled then grew serious. "I thought you two had really hit it off over the past few weeks."

"We did—have—I mean, I enjoy her company," she finished lamely. "And she is definitely no little old lady that needs constant care." But did she want to begin her married life with Antonia in the same house? Other questions nagged her, too. Would Dom feel neglected as she helped her father transition out of the company? How much time alone would they have between their schedules and a third person in the house? Where would they live?

He resided in his boyhood home, and she doubted he would give that up. Honestly, she saw a lot of potential in the old brick row house. But it lacked the view and amenities of her condo. Lake Point Towers had an actual park on the third floor just an elevator ride away, walking trails outside her front door, stores in the building, security around the clock, no maintenance and lakeside.

Then again, the old neighborhood had parks, stores, restaurants, and public transportation within walking distance. And something that excited yet frightened her—families. Lots of them, with backyards that looked over someone else's yard and invited conversation and camaraderie. Dom talked about the neighborhood cookouts and knew the people who lived on his block. His grandparents had lived in the same area; he had strong ties in Lincoln Park. She had to agree it was a much better place to raise a family than a condominium near Navy Pier.

But that was another issue. Did she want a family? Probably, eventually. Right now, she had to focus on James Financial Services. Although she loved Dom, this would be her priority for the next few months.

"Tomorrow is Saturday, our usual date night. Come over around three, and we'll help her go through everything. I'll grill out some steaks then we'll take in a movie, just you and me. How's that?" He put on his fake sexy voice. "I'll make it worth your while."

"Ha! I can see your eyebrows wiggling over the phone." With a sigh, she gave in. "Okay, three o'clock. How many boxes does she have?"

"Only a couple dozen."

Silence.

"I'm kidding! Maybe six total."

Katie rang the doorbell promptly at three. To her surprise, Antonia answered the door and gave her a hug. "*Ciao*, Katie. Nico went out to get some beer for the game tomorrow. He'll be back soon."

They went into the living room where boxes were scattered and opened. Some items lay on the floor while others had not yet been unwrapped. "Where do you want me to start?"

"I'm going through the one on the table. My knees are too old to sit on the floor these days. I can get down but I can't always get up," she said with a wink. "Pick a box, *dolcezza*. Most of the contents are mementos and pictures I will put in my room."

When Antonia turned back around, Katie quickly typed the Italian term into her phone. A term of endearment: sweetie. Warmth spread through her. No one except Dom, Jazzy, and her grandfather had called her anything other than her given name. She heard the click of the radio, and Bing Crosby crooned "White Christmas." They hadn't even bought the turkey yet, and yuletide flooded the airwaves and stores.

"What are your plans for Thanksgiving next week?" Katie had spent many years with Jasmine's family. Her own folks usually went somewhere tropical and golfed over the long weekend. Last year, Dom had cooked for her at the condo.

"I thought I would put on a traditional Italian feast for us. Would you like that?" She looked over her shoulder as she tucked a stray silver lock behind her ear. "I always put up a tree that weekend when I lived here. I hope my ornaments are in one of these boxes. You could help me decorate the tree."

Katie froze. She had never been allowed to decorate the tree as a child. Her mother put on a spectacular holiday display and hired it done. A child's touch would have marred the silver and gold perfection. When she was five, her nanny gave her a tabletop tree to decorate with the homemade snowflakes and stars she made at school. She never put up a big tree as an adult, but the small one from her childhood decorated the top of her mantel every December.

Here was a woman she barely knew, asking her to help decorate a tree with precious keepsakes from decades past. A lump formed in her throat. "That would be wonderful." *Well, I guess I'm here for Thanksgiving.* "Will we have turkey?"

"Of course, but it will be *italiano* style with a secret pancetta paste I smear under the skin, garlic cloves in the neck cavity and a cheesecloth cover soaked in herbs and spices." Her hands demonstrated as she explained then her fingers went to her mouth and made that kissing gesture. "*Delizioso*! I can almost smell it now."

"Sounds fabulous as long as you understand I have no talent in the kitchen whatsoever. Can I bring the wine?"

"You will be my assistant. If you can follow directions, we will make a good team and surprise Nico." She winked and patted her stomach. "You know what they say about men? It is true."

Katie pulled out a rectangular object covered in newspaper. Underneath was a tarnished silver frame with a black and white image of a young couple and a collie. In the distance were snow-capped mountains. They stood in front of an army jeep; a bike with a basket propped against the hood. He had his arm around her, and she leaned into him, her dark shoulder-length hair and plaid dress blowing to one side. Her hand lay affectionately on the dog at their feet. Looking at the stunning young girl, then back at the elderly woman across the room, she gasped. "Is this you and Ken?"

Antonia hurried across the room and with her hands outstretched. "That is what I've been looking for. *Grazie*."

"How old were you there? He's in uniform so it must have been during the war?"

A loving expression flashed across the older woman's face. "It was my eighteenth birthday, and he brought me that bicycle as a gift. I meant to bring this with me on the plane but somehow it got mixed up in the boxes." She gave it a kiss and a private smile spread across her face. "This must go back on the mantel."

"Your dog or Ken's?"

"Dante was our family dog but devoted to me. He followed me everywhere." She looked up at Katie, her eyes gleaming with emotion. "Forgive an old woman a bit of emotion. I have looked at this photograph every day of my life since it was taken. I have missed our daily conversations."

"You talk to the photo?"

"Ah, yes. They are always both right here," she said, a palm over her heart. "It keeps them close when I tell them about my day. Tonight will take a bit longer. We have so much catching up to do."

Katie giggled, feeling like a little girl who'd been let in on a secret. "How did you meet? Did he save you from a burning building? Rescue you from an evil Nazi?"

"Oh no, nothing so exciting as that. Would you like to hear?"

Katie saw the anticipation of a new audience in her eyes. She wasn't a big history fan but World War II had always fascinated her. A time when right and wrong had sharp edges, and the world still held an innocence that considered honor a virtue.

"Please, but let me get us some tea first."

Sitting at the kitchen table with the photo in front of them, the story began. "The Allies had pushed out the Germans and occupied much of Italy. Our little town had survived better than most, and Papa's business reopened a week after the march. Sophia and I returned to town and helped with the café the following month. My sister baked with Mamma and I ran the counter with Papa and waited on tables. Of course, there were only tables since the chairs had been used as firewood..."

Early November 1943

"Get that dog of yours before he chases away our business."

She heard her father yell and rushed out of the kitchen. Another soldier. Dante did not trust anything in a uniform. And who could blame him? They appeared out of monstrous rumbling tanks, loud growling planes, and sometimes with huge snapping parachutes trailing behind them. In their wake, lay a path of destruction. The cathedral still lay in ruins, and piles of rubble dotted the streets and alleys.

"I don't like them either, poor darling," she told the dog, bending down to give him a quick hug then pull him inside as the soldiers approached the storefront. By the uniforms, she identified one British pilot and two American Army airmen.

Sophia swooned every time she saw a bomber jacket. She had dreams of becoming an officer's wife and escaping the poverty of Italy. The war had broken the country, though their family was fortunate in comparison to most. They at least had a roof over their head, an income, and daily meals. Between the café and Guido's business sense, they found the war could turn a small profit for those not shy about taking advantage of a bad situation.

Though her English was good, some of the terms the foreigners used baffled her. But she understood most of the conversation as they approached. "Look, stop beating your gums about it. You're grounded and that's that."

"But I've got more experience than most of those prunes you'll send up in my place. I'm no penguin, I need to fly." The Yank raised his voice in frustration.

"You might rather enjoy being a carrier pigeon, old chap," said the Tommie. "Stop at places like this, pick up favors for the officers, and make a little extra cash."

The Yank with dark hair said something she couldn't understand but she got the gist of it from his tone. "Look, pal. Your ears ain't workin' too good anymore because of all the eggs you dropped. Maybe the hearing will come back if you take some time off. But it's not safe for you or your crew if you can't hear commands."

"Oh blow it out your barracks bag," answered the sandy-haired soldier. "I'll do it but not willingly."

She pulled Dante behind the counter and gave him the quiet sign with her finger to her lips. He sat obediently, alert with ears perked. With a sigh, she faced the men at the counter. "How may I help you?"

"Darlin', that's a loaded question. Lookie here at this little dish," said the Yank with black hair. His smile didn't quite make his eyes, and turned into a

sneer. "I want some of those sticky buns." The way he said "sticky buns" and looked her up and down sent the hair up on her arms.

Dante let out a low growl. "Shhh!"

"Ditto, lass. Get me three," added the thin, shorter Brit.

"You don't eat 'em, Eric. Whatcha doin' with 'em?"

"I trade them for favors, Bob. And to bribe growling dogs, don't ya know?" He turned to Antonia and grinned. "How much?"

"Three hundred lire," she said stone-faced.

"Blimey," he said as he pulled some coins from his pocket. "I hope I don't need it for any mongrels."

The pilot with wheat-colored hair put his elbows on the counter and leaned toward her. "I could buy thirty loaves of bread at home for that much lettuce."

"But you are not home, soldier. You are here, in Benevento, and a sticky bun is 100 lire." She meant to be rude but his soft brown gaze made her heart race as if she'd just chased Dante across the field. His smile went to his eyes, adding crinkles to the corners. Her own lips turned up. "The cost of supplies is very expensive these days, as you know."

"So I've heard. Give me five," he said with a wink. "Maybe I can sweet talk the captain into putting me back into a plane."

"Save your money, Ken. Your ears obviously ain't got any better in the last ten minutes," he answered, rubber-necking over the counter at Antonia's shapely calves. "Get a load of that landing gear."

Dante growled again but this time showed sharp, white teeth. "I don't think he likes you much, Bob."

"Well I don't care for him, neither. Give me two of those, and we'll get out of your hair."

The men paid for the rolls and walked outside. She headed into the kitchen when that quiet, deep voice stopped her. "I'd like to apologize for my friend. He's not a bad Joe once you get to know him."

"I don't think I care to," she said without turning around.

"It looks like I may be making regular trips through your town. Do you work here often?" His tone dripped like honey from a ladle and poured over her; she felt her body turn toward him even as her brain told her "no."

"My family owns it. I am here every day."

"So your father is Guido?" He had resumed his place at the counter, balanced on his elbows again, inviting her back without a word.

She found herself leaning on the counter from the other side. "How do you know my father?"

"The sign says Guido's Café."

She laughed. "Yes, it does. So you are no private eye, eh?"

He whistled then. "You'd make Betty Grable green with envy when you smile. It makes those blue eyes sparkle like a fresh-cut diamond. You should do that more often."

Her eyes lowered, embarrassed at the compliment and the image of the American pinup girl in a bathing suit. "You should go catch up with your friends."

"My name is Ken Lawrence," he said and held out his hand.

"Antonia Capriotti," she replied and took his hand. A tingle shot down her center and curled her toes. "It is nice to meet you."

"You're blushing. Mmm, beautiful and modest. That's a rare find, you know." He held firmly onto her hand. "And who is this?"

She looked down at the silent collie. He hadn't made a noise when this man reached across the counter and touched her. Odd. "Dante, our protector."

"You need one, with mugs like Bob around." He made a kissing noise in the dog's direction and slapped the counter. Dante jumped up, feet on the edge and barked. Ken reached over and scratched the dog behind his ears. "Good boy, you look like my old Schotzie."

"You have a dog?"

"I did. Old man hit fourteen just before I left. Mom sent me his collar when he passed."

"I'm sorry, they are just like one of the family, si?"

"Yes they are," he agreed, giving Dante one more pat before he tipped his hat. "I hope to see you again soon, Antonia."

She hugged the collie as the Yank left, a swagger to his walk. "What do you know that I don't, hmm? I trust your instincts better than mine. Perhaps we'll consider more conversation with this Americano if he returns."

The door opened and Dom's voice called out. "Where are my ladies? Did you finish without me?"

"I'm afraid we got sidetracked," Katie called back with a sigh. "But what happened after that? How long before you saw him again?"

Antonia chuckled. "We will have plenty of time to finish my story. You will come for Thanksgiving next week, si?"

"I have to wait until then?" Dom sat down next to her.

"Your grandmother drives a hard bargain. She leaves me out to dry in the middle of a story, and like any good serial, I don't get the another episode until next week."

"You don't even like romance, and Nonna's specialty is love and drama," he said, ducking as his grandmother's hand swatted at his head. "Storytelling runs in her family. According to Grandpa, her father could spin quite a tale himself."

"No, this is about how she met your grandfather. We had just got to the romantic part. Now I have to wait until turkey day."

"Already talked you into that, did she?" He gave a thumbs-up to his grandmother. "And what about the tree?"

"She agreed to that too, Nico," the old woman said with a wag of her finger. "Katie is much more amenable than you claim."

"What?"

"Now hold on a minute." Dom put his hands in front of him as if warding off a blow. "I just said holidays and cooking aren't really your thing. I never called you disagreeable."

"Well, in his defense, I have never been a big Christmas fan," she said. "You can put your hands down, you're safe."

"We will change that *cara*," Antonia said in low voice. "It is Nico's favorite holiday, and I'm afraid he got that from me."

That night as she lay down to sleep, her mind filled with images of the young couple in front of an army jeep. She could almost hear a dog bark as she drifted off. Thanksgiving couldn't come soon enough.

A kiss is a lovely trick designed by nature to stop speech when words become superfluous.

Ingrid Bergman

CHAPTER SEVEN

The week flew by. Katie dressed with care, casual yet dressy, and inspected her reflection in the mirror. *Jazzy would be proud.* Black slacks with a matching silk blouse embroidered in silver and gold along the collar and cuffs. For some reason, she'd found herself humming Christmas music the past few days and decided to wear something festive. *The Lawrence duo is a bad influence on this Scrooge.*

Slipping on black heels, she grabbed her purse and headed into the kitchen. The wine slid into the red burlap gift bag with a *thunk*. Her stomach flipped a little in excitement. This could be a real family Thanksgiving. If she said yes, they would be her family too.

The tune of "The Christmas Song" emerged from the back of her throat, and the front door locked with a click on her way out. Perhaps she would have a talk with Antonia soon; explain her concerns and see if she had any of her own. It surprised her that the older woman had not mentioned the engagement, or lack of one. As close as Dom was to his grandmother, he would have told her the situation before bringing her back.

The crowded el train, usually void of conversation, buzzed with animated voices straining to be heard over the noise of steel on tracks. Snatches of conversation drifted past. "I almost burned the stuffing…" "I'll be up at three to stand in line for Black Friday to buy…" "Mommy, when does Santa come to the store?" She smiled, surprised that for the first time since childhood, she wanted to watch the Macy's parade on television.

The scent of turkey met her at Dom's front door. For a moment, apprehension swept through her at the thought of helping in the kitchen. Then a handsome man stood before her, and she couldn't wipe the foolish smile off her face. Instead of saying something stupid, she held out the wine.

"In a holiday bag, no less," Dom said, eyebrows raised. He stepped back to let her in, grabbed her hand, and spun her around to face him. "You look stunning."

"I just thought that the burlap would give it extra protection if I dropped it, and they only seemed to have holiday wine bags in stock and—"

One finger covered her mouth. As his head slowly lowered, she could feel his breath on her face; heat raced through her core. By the time their lips touched, her legs had turned to Jell-o; she clung to him for support.

Gently pushing her toward the wall, he pressed his length against her and whispered, "I need to make you mine, legally, before I lose all control. You have no idea the effect you have on me, do you?"

"I think that is the most romantic thing anyone has ever said to me," she said breathless. "Kiss me like that again... please?"

"I'd be happy to oblige if you tell me that isn't my grandmother standing in the doorway watching us."

Katie looked over to see Antonia, a wide grin on her face, and quickly pushed on the hard chest that pinned her to the wall. She ran a hand through her hair as the blood rushed to her face.

"Oh Nico, such good Italian blood in you. And not even any mistletoe out yet." Antonia wiped her hands on her apron and waved to the young couple. "Come now, we have work to do before we play."

The two followed her in like reprimanded children who showed no remorse, holding hands and snickering. *This is silly but it feels so good.* Katie accepted the apron and as she pulled the straps behind her, strong hands covered hers.

"Let me," he whispered in her ear. "I'm good at tying knots."

The pun was not lost on her. His grandmother smiled and busied herself at the stove, humming an old Italian lullaby. She spotted garlic cloves, artichoke hearts, and zucchini on the counter near the sink.

"Could you wash these, *dolcezza*? Slice the zucchini—not too thin— and dice the artichoke." She turned back to some concoction she had simmering on the burner.

Katie washed then dried the vegetables with a paper towel. The knife sliced through the zucchini as easily as the conversation flowed through the kitchen. She found herself enjoying the domestic activity and the closeness of working with loved ones in a small area.

Antonia and Dom had obviously done this before. They both took a taste from the spoon; he reached for salt. He poured it in his palm, sprinkled a pinch across the top, and looked at his grandmother. She nodded and he added a touch more. I am learning more about him in a few weeks through her than in an entire year of dates. Reaching up to pinch her grandson's cheek, she said in a lilting voice, "Wine, wine for the holiday."

Dom quickly retrieved the bottle she had brought, corked it, and put it aside to breathe. She found the wine glasses and set out three. "All done. What can I do next?"

"Take over here, *per favore*." Moving to one side, she handed the wooden spoon to Katie and opened a cupboard door. "Nico, help me get down the custard cups. I don't know why you put things so high up."

"Because I'm six feet and two inches and like to taunt my grandmother." He sidestepped the threatening hand and passed down the glass bowls. "How many? Six?"

"*Si*, we can have more tomorrow."

"Is this custard?" Katie bent over and took in the sweet, pumpkin scent. "It smells divine."

"You are making panna cotta, like a custard. We top it with fruits or sauces but today I used pumpkin for the holiday." Antonia collected the vegetables and began the next dish while Dom poured the wine.

She smiled. *I'm making panna cotta? Where is Jazzy to snap a picture of this?* Pleased with herself, she took the offered wine and made a toast. "To the Lawrences, for turning a James into a cook. Congratulations. This may go down in the family history books."

Laughter erupted and the older Italian put a hand on her cheek. "*Grazie*, but I only need a willing student. Now turn off the fire and pour this evenly into the dishes. Leave a bit of room for the topping."

The next hour passed quickly as they completed preparing the meal. While she set the table, Dom and Antonia finished up the dishes and poured more wine. Teasing and laughter added to the family atmosphere and made her wonder what the gathering would be like with children.

By the time dinner was ready, the trio had drained the bottle and were singing Christmas tunes. As they sat down to eat, she tried to identify the warm and comfortable feeling that filled her. *Contentment.* She was content and relaxed, and embarrassed at the fact that she couldn't recognize the emotion. Instead of introspection, she opted for more wine.

Dom peeled off the cheesecloth soaked in herbs and spices and carved the turkey; the most delicious turkey she had ever tasted in her life. She ate with gusto, listening to her dinner partners reminisce about holidays past. A finger of jealousy tried to wiggle into her happiness but she pushed it away. *No! I will not spoil this moment. I love my family; we just have a different style.*

They decided to wait for dessert and retired to the living room to let their food digest. Within minutes, Dom snored lightly beside her. *It's story time.* "Antonia, could I persuade you to continue the story or are you tired?"

"I am never too tired to think about those days. It pleases me that you ask. Where did we leave off?"

"Ken told you he would be coming through and made friends with Dante." Katie giggled at an answering snore from Dom. "It surprised you because the dog didn't like soldiers."

"Ah, yes. Those were better days in the War. Our poor little café took a beating but was in one piece. Part of the window had shattered and the glass counter cracked when the Americans chased out the Germans. Gunfire shook the town as the tanks roared through, but the bombs missed Guido's café."

Antonia's gaze moved toward the mantel where she had placed the old tarnished frame. "Papa taped the cracks in the counter for extra support. It came on a roll—brown paper, sticky on one side when you wet it—and it made the display case look like an odd jigsaw puzzle. A huge piece of scrap wood replaced the wood on half the storefront. But there was enough glass left to let in some sunlight…"

Late November 1943

"I am ready to muzzle that dog. The noise is driving me crazy," Momma said with a moan. "But as Guido says, those barks turn into lire."

The entire family now helped in the back, leaving no one to stand out front and greet the customers. Dante patrolled the entrance, notifying them if someone approached the door and discouraging any passersby from helping themselves.

"I wish your father would return. It makes me nervous when he goes into Napoli. You never know what can happen along the road." Fedora wrung her hands and peered out the glass section of the storefront. The road to Naples held dangers other than thieves. "Those Nazis left behind enough land mines to blow up the entire boot."

Sophia giggled, "That always makes me think of Italy kicking someone in the backside. I am glad Benevento is in the ankle. I would not like to live in the toe."

"Mussolini has only been able to get in a few little kicks." Her mother made the sign of the cross. *"By the grace of God, we still have one church left."*

Her sister sighed as a jeep drove through the obstacle course of the town, dodging huge chunks of rock and hills of debris collected over the past months. *"I like the soldiers. The uniforms are sexy. Mamma, why I can't I work out front?"*

"Because you think the soldiers are sexy," she said, pinching the girl's cheek hard. *"You would be too busy flirting."*

"Antonia makes eyes at the American soldier. He comes in at least twice a week to see her."

"Ah, but he is the only one she gives any attention. He spends good money each time so your papa allows it." Fedora narrowed her eyes as she studied her oldest daughter. *"Has he asked to see you outside the café yet? Coffee or a walk?"*

"No, Mamma. And I don't know if I would."

"Oh you will, my love, you will. Just make sure to take Dante with you. I remember that look. Guido and I exchanged the same glances and smiled the same smiles." Fedora put an arm around her shoulders and kissed the top of her head. *"We shall add him to our nightly prayers so he does not become another casualty of war."*

The possibility of Ken injured, or worse, sent a sharp pain through her chest. Antonia had lost too much already. She needed to protect herself from more heartache. Her mother was wrong; she would not allow herself to fall for a soldier. Who knew what might happen between now and the end of the war?

Ken did ask her to go for walks, for coffee, for a ride in his jeep, but she refused all offers. His persistence amused her; he now stopped in daily instead of twice a week. She enjoyed his visits immensely, and Guido enjoyed the cash he spent.

Dante picked up on the routine and began meeting him outside of town. He now proudly wore Schotzie's old red leather collar with a small bell on it. Ken would stop the jeep, play with the collie for a bit, and give him a treat. Then both the dog and soldier would ride into Benevento to Guido's. The townspeople noticed the Capriotti dog with the Yank, and the talk began. Whenever she heard the tinkle of the bell, she knew the Yank was not far behind.

"You might as well go with me on a picnic. The whole town thinks we are having an affair anyway. Let's really stir things up." His gray eyes pinned her to the spot as she scrambled to think of a fresh excuse.

"My father would never allow it."

"Your mother would," he argued. "Let's ask her."

"I have a better idea," yelled Fedora from the kitchen. "We will cook for you tomorrow night. Sophia, you may go home early and start the polpette. Guido traded some Strega for sausage."

"But Mamma—"

"You will make the pasta and we still have some broccoli. I haven't decided on the dessert but I'll think of something. It is your birthday, Antonia, we must celebrate."

She'd forgotten. Her heart skipped a beat at spending that special day with this handsome man. If it had not been for the war, her eighteenth birthday would have been a huge celebration, with the half the town in attendance. Ignoring her practical voice, her heart won out and she smiled.

"That's a yes if I ever saw one," hooted Ken, smacking his hands on the counter. Dante went into a barking frenzy, his tail wagging so hard he knocked over the only chair left in the room. "That's right, boy. We've got a date!"

Antonia smoothed out her only good dress. Terribly out of fashion, the heavy cotton fell straight to her calves but the deep violet plaid complemented her dark skin. She added a narrow leather belt, cracked with age, and hoped Ken did not notice. Her black hair hung in waves over her shoulder, brushed to a glossy black.

The sound of the jeep's engine pulled her out of the house. She put a hand over her eyes to see what occupied the passenger side; the sinking sun glinted on metal. Sophia ran down the lane shouting, "It is a bicycle. He has brought it for your birthday."

She stood frozen, unable to speak, as he pulled the shiny silver bike from the vehicle. He rolled it in front of her, looking as proud as any new father. "It should be dry by now. Sorry the color isn't snazzier— we only had aircraft paint. The basket is a bit ragged but it'll work, I think."

"I cannot accept such a gift," she said quietly, tears blurring her vision. "It is too much."

"Now don't snap your cap. Most of the bikes around here were stolen or seized, and this one, just sitting in the corner of a hangar..." he said, palms out in mock defense. "Let me do something for your family to ease my conscience. Our bombs took out most of your beautiful town. This is the least I can do."

"We'll take it," Fedora called out from the window. "But you must eat with us at least once a week in return. Then Guido here cannot say you expect favors from his daughter."

Ken pulled out a camera from behind the seat and handed it to Sophia. "Could you take our picture?" He leaned the bicycle against the jeep and pulled Antonia close to him. Distant barking and a faint jingle sounded from behind the house. He put his thumb and finger in his mouth and gave a shrill whistle. Dante came bounding around the house, slid to a stop in front of the couple, then threw his paws on the pilot's chest.

"Down, boy," she scolded. The dog obeyed but sat between them and leaned into their legs. Her hand automatically sank into the collie's soft fur as Sophia snapped the picture. His arm around her seemed so natural, his touch so familiar, her heart so cold when he let go. Soon the entire family was eager to pose for photographs.

"Eric says a photograph preserves your place in history," the younger girl remarked, handing over the camera.

"I must give you more chores if you have time to talk to that Tommie," Guido yelled as he threw open the front door and walked out, holding Fedora's hand.

Ken clicked the camera at least a dozen times. He posed the girls, the girls and the dog, the parents, then the entire family before announcing emphatically, "This day will be stamped in my memory, an afternoon with the most beautiful family in all of Italy."

Antonia could not remember the last time her family had laughed so much. At least not since the war began. These were the people she remembered growing up with, happy, optimistic and full of life. Ken turned out to be a wonderful storyteller. No matter what the subject, he found a way to add *humor. For a moment, they forgot that misery and death surrounded their little pocket of the world.*

One awkward moment occurred when Fedora called them to the table. There were only two real chairs in the house; the girls each used a stool. Guido saved the day and spotted an old chest. The American never blinked an eye as he pulled it over and escorted the girls to their seat then took a stool, facing them. Antonia silently smiled her gratitude.

He gushed over the modest meal, and complimented the women on their hair and outfits. He discussed the fine art of bartering with Guido, marveling at his shrewdness in business and his ability to provide so well for his family.

"I have made only enough to feed my girls and keep my business open," her father admitted with a defeated look in his eye. "Everything cost so much. Most people, including me, hope to trade but the available goods are scarce."

"Your family is alive and safe. I commend you, Signore Capriotti. You can't ask for more in these times."

The men exchanged a long glance. With renewed vigor, the patriarch slammed his fist on the rough, stained wood. "Wine, woman. Get us more wine! We celebrate tonight!"

Ken patted his belly after the last crumb disappeared from the plates and bowls. "Signora Capriotti, that is the best meal I've had since I left Chicago. I thank you."

Guido grinned. "We have not had dessert. A lemon pie, Antonia's favorite. It is better with cow's milk but we were lucky to hide one goat."

Fedora came out with the lemon pie, the crust a shiny golden-brown. They sang, ate pie, and drank

Strega. When the bottle was half empty, the family called for a song from Antonia. Embarrassed, she shook her head but finally gave in.

In a husky, melodic voice, she sang the Italian love song "Tulipan." The words of romance and hope flowed off her tongue. Looking at Ken, she knew he did not understand the lyrics. Yet his gaze was so intent, she cast her eyes to the floor as pink crept up her neck. At the end of the song, the small audience clapped, and she took a modest bow.

"I hate to break up this shindig but I need to get back to base. Can I help you put the bike away?"

"Antonia, have him put it in the lean-to," her father answered with a yawn. He stood and shook Ken's hand. "You are welcome in our home anytime, Signore Lawrence."

"Thank you sir, I hope to come back soon."

Outside, the moon lit their path as they walked behind the house. He pushed the bicycle between them and she found herself humming the song she had sung earlier.

"You have a lovely voice. I'm not surprised." He took the bike from her and leaned it inside the shelter. He turned before she had a chance to take a step back. Her forehead brushed his chest, and the wings lying dormant in her stomach took flight. As she looked up at him, his hands slowly wrapped around her waist and pulled her closer.

"May I?" he whispered in her ear. His breath tickled her neck and sent Goosebumps down her arms. She felt her insides tremble with anticipation and knew he was about to kiss her.

"I want to but I am afraid."

"Of me?"

"Of us."

"Antonia, I'm crazy about you. I think about you when I wake up and you're in my dreams when I go to sleep. Your smile haunts me if I close my eyes and your voice echoes in my brain." He removed one hand from her hip and tipped her chin up. *"I think it's love."*

"What if you must leave? What if you decide I am not as exciting as your American girls? What if—"

His mouth came down on hers slowly, gently, tenderly. Her head spun as his soft lips claimed hers, then claimed her heart, and claimed her thoughts. Her mind went blank; her body hummed with an urgency she'd never felt. As he pulled away, her chest rose and fell as she tried to catch her breath.

"Yes, I think it is love." She laid her cheek against his hard chest and took in the scent of him. Her world would never be the same.

Katie sat on the edge of the couch with her hand on her heart. "Oh, that is so romantic. And I hate chick flicks."

Antonia nodded. "Yes, it is lovely memory. It makes me think of you and Nico." She glanced over at her sleeping grandson. "You may call me a nosy old woman, and you don't need to answer. Have you thought about marriage?"

The older woman caught her by surprise. Katie was still back in 1943 immersed in a romantic first kiss. "Well, I have thought about it since he proposed last month but—"

"He proposed to you? When?"

"Just before he went to Italy..." It hit her as she recognized the look of surprise on the older woman's face. "He didn't tell you."

"*Per amor del cielo!* Nico, wake up!"

Dom opened his eyes with a jerk. Two women stared down at him, hands on their hips. He swallowed. "Uh-oh."

"Love is like war; easy to begin but very hard to stop."

HL Mencken

CHAPTER EIGHT

What?" he asked innocently. He was stalling because he needed time. *They know! Damn!* "Did I snore too loud? Did I ruin the dessert?"

"You lied to me," Katie began. Her voice slowly rose in pitch as she continued, "How could you not tell your grandmother that you had proposed?"

"Nico, why would you hide such a thing? I asked you if Katie agreed to my coming here."

"Hold on, ladies. I'll address one thing at a time." His hands went up in self-defense and he pulled himself off the couch. Perhaps his height would make them back off. *Nope.* "First, I did not lie to you. I never said I told Nonna about the engagement."

He turned to his grandmother, "I heard the pain in your voice. You would have played the martyr had I told you my engagement was on hold due to my new housemate. True?"

Her eyes fell to the floor, lips tight. "Vero." She quickly recovered. "But that is no excuse to keep us in the dark. We raised you better than that."

"Yes, you did. I planned to resolve all of this, once the two of you had time to get to know one another." He addressed Katie, "You made it perfectly clear that you needed time to think about the arrangement and meet my grandmother. What did it matter if she knew? Did you want her to feel uncomfortable or did you hope she would remain in Italy?"

Katie's horrified eyes told him he'd hit the mark. His father and grandfather had taught him to never initiate an attack but never back down from a confrontation. He stood his ground as the women he loved considered his words.

"I love you both more than anything on this earth. It's a known fact, I don't need to yell it from the rooftops." His voice, quiet but unyielding, now sent a firm message. "I will do everything in my power to have both of you in my life and under my roof. I will entice, coerce, or bully, if need be, to obtain my objective."

He looked at the shocked and silent faces of the females in front of him. His hands on his hips, legs spread out like a male animal in defense mode, he towered over them. "If you feel my motives dishonest in any way, then we need further discussion. Otherwise, it's time for panna cotta."

He bent and kissed each of them forcefully on top their heads then walked into the kitchen, holding his breath until he heard the shuffle of feet and knew they followed. His cheeks puffed out as air escaped his chest. He opened the refrigerator and took out three small bowls of the pumpkin dessert.

"Get the gingersnaps I crushed up earlier for the topping. And a bottle of Strega. We all need a drink," Nonna said at his shoulder. The crisis had ended for now; he heard it in her voice. "Katie, will you come tomorrow and help me decorate the tree? Nico will put it up tonight before he goes to bed."

He smiled. Yes, his grandmother understood but what about Katie? Her pragmatic mind would need longer to absorb and analyze the situation. Fine. He had plenty of time. She gave a dazed nod to Antonia.

The three sat down at the table, the festive mood dampened. Antonia poured glasses of the yellow liquid and made a toast. "I do not always agree with the men in my life. They are often stubborn, hardheaded, and I could not love them more. Dominic has proved to be a true Lawrence today. *Saluti!*"

An unwilling smile hovered on Katie's mouth. Dominic saw the battle of emotions cross her face. Slowly, she raised her glass. "*Saluti!*"

The trio enjoyed dessert while Christmas tunes played in the background. His grandmother told stories of family traditions and Katie joined in with some of her own. They talked about Vincenzo and the Romanos in New York. The families always took turns celebrating in either New York or Chicago until his folks died. Now he usually spent a few days in the Big Apple.

"Nonna, where shall we spend Christmas Eve this year? Would you like to go to New York?"

"Vincenzo called yesterday. It would be nice, but I think this first year back, I would like to stay here, at home."

Katie stifled a yawn. When she announced it was time for her to go, his offer to drive her home was graciously rejected.

"I need some time to put this into perspective," she said as he walked her to the el train. "Not just because you didn't tell her about us but the whole subject of marriage. I'm relieved she didn't know. I wondered if perhaps she didn't care if her presence threatened our relationship."

"Nonna sees something warm and genuine in you, but she also sees fear." He stopped her with a gentle hand on coat sleeve. "What are you afraid of?"

"Everything, nothing. I'm realizing that I'm the problem, not you or Antonia. Since the night I put our lives on hold, I've found myself in virgin territory, emotionally. You have such a history with your extended family in New York... The thought of being wrapped in the cocoon of a larger-than-life Italian family thrills me and terrifies me. I need to figure out answers to all the questions bouncing around in my head." Tears filled her eyes and he wiped one away with his thumb. "Where will we live? How will we manage our crazy schedules and still find time for just us? What about kids—"

"We can work it out together. Why are you so insistent on figuring it out on your own?" he asked, pulling her close and cradling her head against his chest. "Don't you feel this? The beating of my heart, the love surrounding us... This is what matters, not the logistics."

She held him tight, and he placed a soft kiss on her neck, just inside her woolen scarf. Her warm skin trembled under his lips. "Dom, I don't think I deserve you. I don't know if I'd make a good mother, or if I can do the whole domestic neighborhood scene, but I'm not ready to give up the idea."

He had to be satisfied with that for now. The whole incident had gone better than expected and the tactician in him said to back off. "I'm at the bar with the guys tomorrow. If you want me to come home before you finish with Nonna, just text. I'll only be a couple blocks away."

His grandmother met him at the door. "She's a tad skittish, eh?"

Dom nodded. "I'm sorry, I should have told you but with the funeral and the packing—"

"You do not need to apologize when you do things out of love, *caro*." Her leathered hand patted his cheek. "What did Katie say?"

He gave her the gist of the conversation as he got out another dessert cup and reheated the coffee. "I'm sure my ears will be ringing while she and Jazz are on their Black Friday adventure."

"She loves you, I can see it in her face. You bring a brightness to her eyes when she looks at you or hears your voice. Her life will be lonely without you in it. That spark will die, and she will grow cold again." With a sigh, she perched on the edge of the couch and seemed lost in thought.

"Grandpa adored you, Nonna, and I understand that now. This kind of feeling is rare and it's worth fighting for. I don't know if it's the Lawrence determination or the Capriotti stubbornness but I can't let her go."

"I might have ended up like her if it had not been for Ken. Such persistence." She patted his knee. "Don't give up, Nico. Her family upbringing was different. Not bad but very different, and I see her trying to break free. She is a redhead, you need to stoke that fire. But first, you must put up the tree so we can decorate it tomorrow."

Katie carefully pulled out each ornament from the box and set it carefully on the table. The tree was a perfect replica of a scotch pine and stood by the fireplace. The mantel already had greens and twinkling white lights. Antonia attached tiny clear icicles to the branches and they sparkled in the glow.

"In that box is my nativity scene," she pointed to the taped cardboard on the couch. "My mother bought it for my first Christmas in the states and I have used it every year since."

The wooden stable stood about a foot tall and included several built-in stalls and straw glued to the roof. The different shades of yellow indicated where new straw had been added over the years. Hand-carved, painted figures of Mary, Joseph, and baby Jesus in a cradle were wrapped in newspaper and laid inside the shelter. Three wise men, buried at the bottom beneath a menagerie of barn animals, carried gifts for the infant.

"It's beautiful, I've never seen one so detailed," she exclaimed, pulling out each piece. "Shall we put it in the dining room as the center piece or the coffee table?"

"Olivia, Nico's mother, always liked it on the coffee table so the children could see it."

"What? You let kid play with this?" She knew how expensive it would be to replace a set like this. Katie's mother would have kept it well out of reach.

"Of course. It is how we instilled a love of the story. We would act out the night of our savior's birth. The children loved it. Nico and Vincenzo always fought over being the wise men. When they thought we weren't looking, the boys would give the animals voices and make up their own version," the elderly woman said with a chuckle. They arranged the pieces inside and out of the miniature barn together.

"Is Christmas in Italy much different?"

"The customs are not all similar but the atmosphere and mood is the same." She headed into the kitchen. "Could you get the lights on the tree for me while I pour some wine?"

As they worked, marveling at some of the antique ornaments, Katie found a serenity replacing the tension in her stomach. She knew her first attempt at tree lights looked pitiful, but Antonia insisted she did a fine job. Globes, snowmen, angels, and stars filled the holes in her haphazard lighting and strings of silver icicles did the rest. It did look beautiful!

Unwrapping the last few objects, Katie found an old red dog collar made of leather with a small jingle bell attached. "Aw, this must be Dante's?"

"Oh, *si*. Let me have it." She placed it on a lower branch of the tree. "This was his spot by the tree. He seemed to think he needed to guard the presents and slept in the same place every year."

"So he came here with you?"

"Dante was the reason I took a chance on Ken. That collie never liked another soldier but him. His dog Schotzie died during the war, and he knew it would break my heart to leave him behind."

Antonia sat down at the table, leaning heavily on her elbows. "Let's rest for a moment."

"What about the bell? Did it keep him from chasing animals? Jazzy puts one on her cat's collar to warn the birds."

"Clever, but no. Ken gave the collar to Dante in Benevento. Such a pair, those two. That dog had an innate sense of when his friend was close. He'd disappear and when he returned jingling that bell, I knew Ken wasn't far behind. It gave me time to check my face and brush my hair."

"Will you tell me the rest of the story now? I hated the way we stopped yesterday. I'm so sorry," Katie had wanted to say that since she'd arrived. In a few short weeks, she had grown so fond of Antonia that the thought of hurting this dear woman consumed her with guilt. "I am so glad you came home with Dominic and we've had a chance to get acquainted."

"Me, too, *dolcezza*," she said softly, and reached out for her hand. "I will tell you the end of our story—in Italy. I think it will help you in the decision you must make."

"But—"

"Let an old woman have her say," she said in a tone that brooked no argument. "It was Christmas Eve and we had not expected him to come..."

December 24, 1943

"How did you manage to get away?"

"Some of the fellas owe me a few favors," Ken *whispered loudly, the back of his hand on the side of his mouth. "I don't have long but I'm on a mission from Santa."*

The family stared at the Americano's bag. None of them, especially Antonia, had expected presents for Christmas. Being alive for another holiday had been a gift in itself. He pulled a fake white beard from the paper sack and put it on, the elastic going around his head and laying on top of his ears. Over this went the red hat trimmed in flattened white cotton.

"I know it's not the best costume, but you get the picture." The airman laughed as the family stared at him in disbelief. He set a small oval object, wrapped in newspaper, on the table.

No one had the heart to tell him that Italians preferred La Befana to St. Nick. Antonia giggled. Her handsome pilot would look very silly dressed up as an old woman with a broomstick. Her parents gasped as Fedora unwrapped the "family" present.

"I know it's not much but I thought you'd enjoy a taste of an American holiday meal. I had a heck of a time sneaking out my plate." He reached down and gave a Dante a good scratch behind the ears. "My buddy here already got his ham scrap when he met me at the bottom of the hill."

Sophia clapped her hands together. "It's turkey and mashed potatoes, ham and pumpkin pie. I'll get the forks!"

His generosity touched them, each in a different way. Sophia pulsed with excitement, Fedora cried and hugged him, Guido remained curiously silent and pumped his hand up and down, and Dante continued to lick the remnants of ham from his fingers.

The wall around Antonia's heart cracked open. Rather than tears, she felt a pride that this kind, extraordinary man loved her. She threw her arms around his neck and squeezed him tight. "You are the best part of Christmas, my American Santa. Grazie."

After the small plate of goodies disappeared, amid groans and moans of delight, the happy group sat in front of the small fire and sang. First, the Capriottis sang an Italian favorite, then Ken would teach them the chorus to an American favorite. The hour flew by and the family watched him stand, regret on their faces.

Ken stood in front of them, looking at the floor, mouth open as if searching for words. "I... I leave on a mission right after Christmas. I don't know exactly when and I can't say where. My hearing is good again and I've got my wings back."

Antonia stopped breathing. The room swam before her; she closed her eyes to stop the spinning. He could not leave her now. Not now. Her heart had just convinced her to love him. Her mother reached over and gave her arm a shake, and she sucked air into her lungs as a cry escaped her lips. "NO! No, no..." Her hands covered her face as the tears streamed down her face.

"I'll be back, I promise," he looked from her to the rest of the family, pleading for each one to believe him.

"Oh, sure, sure. Of course you will." Guido jumped up and slapped the taller man's shoulder. "We'll see you soon."

Fedora hugged him. "And you will write. We will all write, si?"

"Yes, letters. There will be so many letters," added Sophia, her voice cracking. "We will need a paper mill to keep up."

Both women wrapped their arms around him at the same time. When they finished, Guido gave the man a huge bear hug. "The lord will watch over you. Fe, run and get the medal of St. Michael. Ken will keep it until he returns."

When her mother hurried back, the medal dangling from its chain, Antonia's tears stopped. She moved forward, took it from her, and turned back to Ken. He bent his head as she extended her arms and carefully placed the tarnished silver around his neck, painstakingly tucking the medallion inside his shirt. With a pat on his silver uniform buttons, she swallowed back another sob and gave him a bright, glistening smile.

"We will be together again, I feel it here," she murmured softly, her hand grasping at the pocket

over her heart. Then in his ear: "Do not ever think I regret what has passed between us. Our memories will keep me company until you return."

She saw the grief in his eyes and knew, whatever happened, some greater force connected them. No matter the future, her heart would never lament loving this man.

"Will you and Dante walk me down the lane?" He took her hand and grabbed the paper sack with his costume in the other. She grabbed her faded, wool coat and wrapped the matching olive scarf over her head.

Outside, they strolled in silence down the hill. Dante moved in front of them, stopping often to let them catch up

"You must take the collar with you, in case..."

"No, I gave it to Dante. Nothing on God's green earth will keep me from coming back to you."

"But if something did happen—"

"I'll compromise." At the bottom of the hill, Ken squatted down and slapped his hand on his thigh. "Come here, boy."

The dog obediently sat in front of the soldier as he removed the bell from the collar. It clinked as the dog tried to lick his hand. "I'll take half and you keep half." He stood and wiped a stray tear from her cheek before he continued, "When I come back, I'll put this on again myself."

She opened her mouth but he stopped her with a kiss. It filled their hearts with so much more than any words could. The urgency of their love spilled between them—hands and lips moving in haste, a searing taste of what might be, a promise of now. With one deep breath, his scent etched into her brain; something to cling to in their uncertain future. His eyes roamed over her, a man hungry for memories in the long nights ahead. She saw his gaze stop on each feature of her face, making notes and remembering each line, each soft curve, for a lifetime.

"Marry me. I have another day or two. Let's make it legal and tie the knot before I go."

Antonia shook her head. "No, I do not want a proposal out of panic. When you come back to me, ask me again. I will say yes."

He kissed her like he said the movie stars did, leaning her backwards and almost sweeping her off her feet. She thought of the first time they met when he compared her to one of the American pinup girls.

"When you hear this," he said, his voice raw as he rattled the bell in front of her, "you'll know I'm only a moment away. I'll count the days, then the hours and the minutes, Antonia." He wrapped his strong arms around her and kissed the top of her head. "I have to go."

She kneeled down and gripped Dante's neck as his shadow moved into the empty night. Her heart, as dark and heavy as the cold winter air, ached with each rise of her chest. "We will seem him again, Dante. Tell me, we will see him again."

His soft whine broke her reserve, and she sobbed into the collie's fur, holding onto the dog for dear life.

If you live to be hundred, I want to live to be a hundred minus one day so I never have to live without you.

A.A. Milne

CHAPTER NINE

"He left you? For how long?" Katie stared at the older woman who had just grown two heads. "How does this help me make any decisions?"

"Obviously, he did not leave me forever," she answered and looked toward the heavens. "Dammi la pazienza!"

A chill swept through the room as Dominic opened the door and called out in warning, "I'm home!"

"Oh, that's great timing," Katie mumbled. "I'm not waiting for another installment. I need to hear the end."

"The end of what?" He dodged the napkin and stray piece of garland the ladies shot in his direction. "Oh, the war-torn love saga?"

Antonia beamed. "Yes, Nico. I was about to finish my story but she became impatient and interrupted me."

Katie tried to look remorseful but failed miserably. "Okay, I'll shut my mouth until you say 'The End', deal?"

"Deal. Now where was I?" Katie saw the impish light in her eye and knew she teased. "Ah, yes. I did not see him again throughout the war. We did exchange letters. As Sophia promised, we all wrote. Papa did some heavy bartering to keep us in paper but still we often used parts of brown bags and whatever scraps we could find.

"Hitler had surrendered but the Japanese continued to fight..."

Early May 1945

"Almost one million men surrendered yesterday, May 2 to the British," Guido read from a newspaper a soldier had brought to the café. "This happened right on the tail of Hitler's suicide, 29 of April, during the Battle of Berlin."

Antonia didn't know whether to scream with joy or cry. Could it be over? Sophia decided for both of them as she hooked an arm in her sister's and twirled them both around the front of the shop. " Evviva! Evviva!"

As the news spread, the main street of Benevento filled with its remaining inhabitants. The hope and happiness floated through the air, so thick she wished she could grab a handful and send some to Ken...

Her bliss fizzled away with the breeze, the sun beat down on her head, and a trickle of sweat worked its way down her back. She had not heard from him in six months. The letters had come at least monthly until the end of last year. She did not know if he had been injured, killed, or found someone else—and wasn't sure which would cause her more heartache.

The Capriottis had studied the Allied troops' movements closely after Ken left. Shortly after his letters stopped last December, they read about the Battle of the Bulge and the immense losses. A last Italian campaign had been fought in April. Could he have been in one of those?

Sophia asked her British soldier, Eric, daily for news of Ken. The answer was always the same: he had no access to intelligence and if he did, they would not be privy to the information. The sympathetic airman always added his apologies and promised to let them know if the American's name appeared on any lists.

By late May, Antonia could not bear for her sister to ask again. The futile question only added to the pain and made everyone uncomfortable. She kept a cheery face and cried into Dante's smooth, comforting fur each night. He missed the man as much as she did. If time could be reversed, she would have married him. Better a widow with a barracks bag of memories than this uncertainty.

One morning in early June, she hung the family's laundry to dry in the sun. He father had made some pins from salvaged wood and using them, she added a pair of her father's pants to the line. The scent of bougainvillea was heavy in the air and the sky a clear blue without one cloud.

Dante took off, probably chasing another rabbit. At four, his muscles were in peak condition and the dog could almost outrun the wild hares. Hands on her lower back, she leaned back and stretched her sore muscles. A sound, like the tinkle of a bell, caught her attention.

Her body seemed paralyzed while her mind raced; her ears strained for the sound again. Another delicate clink on the next breeze. With a racing heart, she straightened up and shielded her eyes from the sun. The dreaded wings in her stomach took flight, and her hands clutched at her middle, trying to hold down her breakfast. Over the hill, Dante galloped toward her at full speed, the little bell jangling madly from his collar.

Her feet moved without any instruction. At the bottom of the hill, stood a lone figure. Something on his chest glinted in the sun and the man took off his military cap and waved. Antonia's legs were rubber and seemed to move in slow motion. Tears streamed down her cheeks, almost stumbling once, but she never took her eyes off the image below for fear it would disappear.

He ran with the speed of an athlete and barely broke stride as he slowed, scooped her up and continued up the hill. His lips trailed kisses across her face, her eyes, her neck. Her lips. He covered her mouth with a groan, and her lids squeezed tightly shut as she kissed him back. After a long, tender moment, he pulled back.

"Open your eyes, Antonia. I need to see those gorgeous blues that kept me going the past two years."

She shook her head, drops falling over the thick lashes. "I might wake up. I don't think my heart will survive if this is a dream."

Then her mother and sister came out, yelling and singing and dancing, and she knew it was no dream. When she saw the happiness mixed with the pain and horror of war in those loving grey eyes, she knew he needed to heal. And she would gladly nurse him for a lifetime.

Katie took a kleenex from her purse, dabbed at her eyes, and blew her nose. "Oh my, that should be a movie. It really should."

Dom blinked his eyes and gave a light sniff. "That ending gets me every time. And I know it's coming!"

Antonia smiled, stood up, and walked to the mantel. "Now do you understand why I talk to this photograph every day?" They nodded. "Nico, why do you not have a dog?"

Dom looked at the collar hanging on the lower branch of the tree. "My schedule hasn't allowed it. I've worked such long hours, expanding the business. It didn't seem fair to buy one if I couldn't spend time with it. But now that you're here..."

His grandmother smiled in agreement. "That would be nice, *cara*. We should think about it. Now, would you be a good boy and make me a cup of tea?"

His eyes narrowed, as if he suspected something, then left the two women at the table.

Katie took advantage of the time alone. "So the moral to this story is... grab true love when you can?"

"I suppose. You could think of several themes along that line. Instead, I want you to ask yourself something."

Antonia sat down and took one of Katie's hands in hers, turned it over and traced the lifeline on her palm. "You have many years ahead of you, *dolcezza*, but each one is a precious gift, and they fly by much too quickly. How would you feel if Nico walked out that door, and you never saw him again? Could you go on and find happiness with another?"

She had not expected an inquiry. Her heart lurched at the thought of Dom disappearing from her life. Perhaps this clever woman had a point. Had she been trying to find the answers to the wrong questions?

Yesterday, Dominic had watched his girlfriend hang on Nonna's every word and thought back to their last conversation. Katie admitted the extra time since the proposal had given her the opportunity to consider issues they hadn't discussed. His grandmother had also made her take a long look at the reasons for her reluctance. His time was coming; he could feel it.

As visions of children and family barbecues danced in his head, an idea began to form. Over the next two weeks, he searched through the online rescue sites and newspapers. Perhaps a wiggly little canine would get Katie's maternal juices flowing. Nonna would appreciate the company during the day and he missed having a dog around. But he needed to find just the right puppy for all of them. The James' never celebrated Christmas Eve, so Katie planned to spend the evening with him and Nonna. Jazz agreed to help with his plan under the condition she accompanied him on all puppy inspections.

"Does it have to be a collie?"

Dominic considered this. "No, but at least a collie mix to look the part. If I don't totally blast her with romance, it won't work. Plus, it has to be perfect for Nonna, too."

"Dang, I wish you had a brother."

"I have a cousin," he answered, with a wiggle of his thick brows.

"Yeah, he's pretty hot but too much of a player for me." Jazz flipped her blonde hair and dismissed the subject with a sigh. "I wish you'd let me record this. It's only fair, since I'll be cleaning up puppy messes until Christmas Eve."

Three days before Christmas Eve, he was ready to give up. His secretary knocked and poked her head around the door. Line two, one of those animal shelters again. He crossed his fingers, shook his head at the ridiculousness of that, and picked up the phone. "Lawrence here."

"Hi, Dominic Lawrence?"

"Yes?"

"I had your name on our list for a collie or collie mix. We just finished up an investigation, a hoarder, and we have a female collie with four pups about four months old," she paused. "I know it's close to the holiday and many people go out of town but if you have time to come in and take a—"

"What time do you close?"

Christmas Eve arrived with giant snowflakes falling from the heavens. The streets of Lincoln Park looked clean and peaceful. He had picked up Katie earlier, pleased that she'd handed him a shopping bag of gifts to carry. "Just a few things I picked up this week that made me think of Nonna."

Hearing her use of the endearment, *Nonna*, for his grandmother sent holiday cheer running through his veins. The two women had spent several Saturday nights together, wrapping presents or watching the sappy movies on the holiday countdown. Jazz had been invited and reported that he was not the main topic of discussion.

"Shall I top off our wine and pass out the gifts?" Dominic looked at his watch. Less than half an hour. He wanted to get this over with and eliminate the knot in his stomach. Maintaining a blank face was not an easy task for his Italian side.

"Sure, Nico. I can tell you're anxious. Are you expecting a special gift?" Nonna grinned at him and nodded, as if to say, *"You can't put anything past me."*

He screwed up his face to keep from smiling, like a silly schoolboy with a secret, and escaped to the kitchen for wine. Maybe he'd down this bottle while no one watched, and open another one. Liquid courage. *Clear head, buddy. Keep a clear head.*

Katie took out the packages in her bag and divided them into piles. He went to throw away the empty bag but saw a gift still inside. "Did you forget one?"

"No, I thought I might stop by Jazzy's on the way home. Would you mind?" She misread his hesitation and quickly added, "No big deal if you're tired. We can exchange later."

Dominic went to the closet and got out the fluffy, white beard, jacket, and hat. As he passed the mirror, the thought crossed his mind that at least three generations of Lawrences had dressed up as Santa to pass out packages to their families. He said a little prayer to his folks that he might produce a fourth.

Katie almost spilled her wine when he stepped back into the room. "You are the skinniest, tallest St. Nick I've ever seen." She stood on her toes and gave him a kiss. "And the most handsome."

"Just for that, Ms. James, I'll give you something special," he replied in his best Santa voice. "I hope you like dolls."

Another giggle. "A Ken doll would be nice. That would make my Barbie and me very happy."

Ripped and crumpled wrapping paper soon littered the floor. Nonna loved her new robe, e-reader, bottle of wine, and espresso machine. Dominic exclaimed over his football sweatshirt and cap, hockey coffee table book, socks, and running shoes. Katie insisted that the afghan would match her bedspread to a tee, the watch exactly the one she had pointed out on a shopping trip, and the gift certificate for a spa day divine.

Looking out the window, Dominic saw a scarf disappear up the front steps. *She's here. Give her time to get the key in the lock and down the hall.*

"I do have one more present." That got their attention. "It's a little something for both of you, if you don't mind sharing."

"What could we share?"

"It can't be clothes."

"Maybe it's more wine."

He slapped his forehead as they both fell into a fit of giggles. "Shhh! Listen!"

In the silence, they heard the door open. A bell jingled, first faintly then louder. Nonna gasped and covered her mouth as a small collie ran into the room. Around his neck, he wore Dante's collar with the bell. "If Ken's ghost walks through that door next, I'll have a heart attack."

"No, this time it's Katie's turn." He crouched near the floor and slapped at his thighs. The puppy trotted over to him. He lifted him gently onto Katie's lap.

"Hello, there little one. And what's your name? You look like Dante." She put his head between her hands and rubbed them up and down the puppy, then stopped.

It was the moment he had planned for weeks. Again. The questioning look from her, his nod, the shaky fingers as she tried to take the small package tied on the collar. "Let me help with you that," he said, his tone gruff with emotion as he handed her the small box.

"Dom, I..." She peeled off the paper to find a familiar black velvet box. Her eyes filled with tears, her lips trembled. He took it gently from her hands and opened it once more.

"I have been a patient man but I do not want to spend one more day without you. So we'll try this one more time." He lowered one knee, held out the box, and asked, "Kathleen James, you are the love of my life. Will you marry me and let me spend the rest of my years making you happy?"

Slowly, she put the dog on the floor. Her eyelashes, wet against her skin, made dark halos on her cheek. When she looked up, her gaze held no doubt, no hesitation, no remorse. She simply said, "Yes," and threw her arms around him.

Jazzy did a happy dance and Nonna began to sing "Hallelujah." Little Dante had no idea what had happened but joined in the celebration with a bark and chased his tail.

Antonia looked up at the mantel, the frame illuminated by the dancing flames of the fire, and quietly spoke to Ken, "Another bell, another perfect love. May they be as happy as we were and for just as long."

The End

Note from the Author

When I began writing this story, I wanted the setting and details to be as accurate as possible. For part of my research, I consulted with my stepfather, Eric Merry. A British World War II veteran, he was stationed first in North Africa and then Italy. His suggestions added an authenticity to the story I could have never achieved on my own.

He recommended Benevento as the setting. The town retains its charm today and I hope to visit there on my trip to Italy. Sticky buns were a popular treat for the American soldiers and the liqueur Strega continues to be an important part of the city's heritage.

Be sure to check out the links below to an old newsreel link, showing the American soldiers entering the bombed city, and more information on the ancient and lovely town of Benevento. I also included the recipe for panna cotta. It's one of my favorites.

Information on Santa Sofia, Benevento:
https://en.wikipedia.org/wiki/Santa_Sofia,_Benevento
World War II footage
https://www.youtube.com/watch?v=-2RXMn7kJoo
Strega
https://en.wikipedia.org/wiki/Strega_(liqueur)

Pumpkin panna cotta with crushed gingersnaps:

http://www.meals.com/recipe/pumpkin-spice-panna-cotta-145236

COMING SOON

Excerpt from Rolf's Quest

Prologue

Caledonia Forest, Scotland
Autumn, 1139

The ancient limbs of the Rowan groaned as a strong wind tunneled through the Forbidden Forest. "By the gods, Vivien, if I get out of here you will pay," Merlin raged, his long, white beard trembling with fury. A flutter of leaves danced and spiraled, falling between the gnarled roots that pushed through the dense carpet of sticks and bark.

The raspy voice echoed and bounced off the thick trunks of the trees as if to mimic the sorcerer's threat. Vivien was nowhere near the legendary forest, and the old man only ranted at an innocent squirrel resting on a sturdy branch. The centuries had slowly chipped away at his patience, replaced by a grim determination to overcome the curse she'd placed upon him.

The snap of a branch caught Merlin's attention. He stilled at the sound of horses. "Where have you been? Do you no longer find it necessary to heed my summons?" His voice cracked, and the wind again picked up, blowing around bits of debris and restricting his view.

Two shadowy figures emerged from the gloomy interior of the forest. A taller man on a large stallion dwarfed the boy who sat on a smaller pony. They came to a stop before him, the horses' nervous prance crunching the dead leaves under their hooves. The man dismounted, his mail chinking softly as his feet hit the ground. "Baron Giles Arbrec at your service, my lord."

"Why does it take so long to answer my call?" The wizard spoke softly but the tone was deadly. "Do you no longer fear my wrath?"

"Merlin, I have come as commanded." He knelt before the tree, head bowed, broad shoulders rippling under his hauberk as he bowed his head. "It is the boy's tenth name day. I proudly present my first–born and only son, Rolf Arbrec." The baron looked over his shoulder. "Dismount boy. Come pay homage to Merlin."

The youngster's wide, amber eyes looked to either side then back at his elder as he joined him. "Father, there is no one here. You are talking to a tree."

A haze appeared in the center of the trunk then transformed into a face. Merlin gazed at the boy and felt a small crack in what was once his heart.

"Are you..." Rolf put his shoulders back and his chin up. He cleared his throat and asked again in a clear voice, "Are you the mighty wizard of legend?"

The snowy whiskers rippled with the rusty sound of his chuckle. "Indeed I am. And pleased to hear that my feats are still spoken of after such a long absence."

"Kneel, Rolf, and show your respect." The baron slapped his son on the chest with the back of his hand.

"He is a fine–looking lad." Merlin studied the frightened boy who tried so desperately to hide his fear. "Leave him. We have much to teach him and little time to do it."

"I cannot abandon him here in the Caledonia Forest," exclaimed Baron Arbrec, rising to his feet and waving a fist in the air. "He is all I have left.

Calmness blanketed the sorcerer for the first time in centuries. This boy was the one. He could see it in the intensity of his gaze and the determined set of his jaw. "What else would you have me do, Arbrec? He is our last hope. This Rowan is dying and me along with it. If the curse is not broken before the last bloom of this tree, we are all doomed for eternity."

"Curse? Upon our family or upon you?" Curiosity replaced Rolf's fear.

Good sign. "You are my family, boy. I am saddened this responsibility must fall on such young shoulders, but you will be my champion. It will be your name the folk will one day whisper."

"But I am to blame for this tragedy. Why must my only son suffer the consequences?"

The wizard gave a long, tired sigh. "In truth, I am at fault, and many generations have paid for my sins. You came so close to ending this, Giles. If you had only married his mother... But even a battle-hardened soldier of great valor has his fears."

The excitement in the boy's eyes faded as the ground shook with the old man's disappointment. Another gust of wind sent more leaves tumbling to the ground. The boy steadied himself with both hands in the dirt but raised his head to Merlin. "I am at your command."

"Stand, my son, and bid your father farewell." The baron's hands shook as he removed a chain from his neck and placed it over Rolf's dark head. A plum-colored stone flashed with strands of brilliant violet as it landed gently on the narrow chest.

"Wear this amulet at all times. It will keep you safe." Arbrec nodded toward the image in the tree. "He will protect you until you have completed your task. Forgive me for my failure." He gripped the slender boy in a fierce hug.

When their eyes met, Merlin felt Arbrec's agony like a stone in his gut. "You may visit each solstice and see how he fares. I am not a monster."

Arbrec nodded. "I will regret my mistake for the rest of my days. Watch over him. He is my life." Pushing his son away firmly, he turned his back and walked to his horse. The boy wiped his tear-stained cheeks with the back of his dirty hands but stood his ground and did not run after his father.

Damn you again, Vivien. Rolf will find genuine love, without the use of trickery, and she will return that tenderness. Then your day of reckoning will arrive.

Merlin watched as the boy silently waved to the retreating figure, a shadow fading into the darkness of the forest. His features softened and kindness shown in the faded eyes. "You have great courage and strength, Rolf. I will teach you things beyond your imagination. We shall help each other, you will see."

CHAPTER ONE

England
Early December 1154

Melissa fidgeted in the saddle as her gloved fingers wrapped and unwrapped around the reins. She swung her feet in the stirrups and created a dull monotone beat between the horse's blanket and her heavy skirts. The landscape provided little color with its yellowed fields and bare branches. She made a sign of the cross and thanked St. Agricola for the mild weather and clear sky during this trip. It never mattered how many layers of wool she wore when riding all day in a wintry drizzle. It always chilled one to the bone.

They had traveled for three days on rutted roads and crude paths suffering three days of uncomfortable beds, bad food, and her mother's constant chatter about her duties as a wife. She needed an escape, a few moments alone to calm her nerves.

Her father, the Earl of Garrick, rode ahead with his small army, determined to make London before the end of the week. She smiled with pride as he rode up and down the lines of his men. He spoke to one knight, reprimanded another, and then laughed with his steward. She prayed her future husband would be as commanding and respected as her father.

The trip to London served two purposes. They would attend the coronation of Henry Plantagenet, and she would meet her betrothed, Charles Whitburn. As the Duke of Sunderland, his title and family connections could improve her father's holdings and position at court. After obtaining royal approval, they would hold the ceremony. Two wagons followed with her personal items and dowry.

"Melissa, did you hear me?" her mother asked sharply.

She nodded, but the words drifted away on the late autumn breeze. Even her horse's head drooped low when Lady Agnes's high–pitched voice began again. Her hand instinctively reached out and rubbed the gelding's neck. "Just a few more days, Thunder. We are almost there."

"Your time would be better spent listening to me than talking with that beast," Lady Agnes chided. Then seeing her daughter's frown, she held up a hand in surrender. "I will give you some respite since you refuse to pay me attention. What is going on in that lovely mind?"

"Do you remember the day father signed my marriage contract?" As a young girl of ten, Melissa had met the former duke. She recalled his blond, wavy hair and warm brown eyes. He had seemed a giant of a man as he smiled down at her and asked her to turn in a circle. Then, looking at her father, he had simply said, "Yes, she'll do."

Melissa reached over the gap between their horses and clutched her mother's arm. "Do you think Charles will look like his father?"

"We can only hope, child. It will make your nights much more pleasant." She shook her head, a perplexed look on her face. "Such a handsome man to die in such a way. Yet it did expedite this union."

"The letter said an arrow pierced his heart and another went through his eye. Yet they have no clue about those responsible." Melissa shivered delicately. "Why do they not think he may have been set upon by thieves?"

"Neither the purse of silver nor the horse was taken. The Scots claimed it must have been a random hunter who did not realize where his arrows landed." Agnes gave an indelicate snort. "The duke had influence in the court of Henry I. It looks like the family may rise again now that Henry's grandson has reclaimed the throne. Be happy you are at least joined with a young man on the right side of the throne. I only wish his lands were not so close to the border and those savages."

"I am not foolish enough to pine for a love match," Melissa answered. "But I do want an opportunity to get to know him before we are wed. Is this too much to ask?"

"My dear, you will have a lifetime for that. If he resembles his father in more than just appearance, you may consider yourself fortunate indeed. And we will be in London for a month. You will have sufficient time to learn more about your husband."

"When did you first meet Father?"

"Our marriage was performed by proxy. I met him the day my family delivered me to his gate. The man that stood in his place reeked of onion and had a belly that fell over his belt." Agnes chuckled. "I felt more relief than fear at the first glimpse of my husband."

"And you have been happy?" She watched her mother's face for any signs of regret but saw none.

"My mother trained me well how to manage a house and lands. I have assumed your father's responsibilities on many occasions when he left to defend our lands or fight for our King." Her chin went up. "I can settle disputes, oversee finances, and defend our castle, if needed. Your father and I hold a mutual respect for one another. I am content with my life."

"And this is what I should I hope for?"

"Yes, my love. That is all you can hope for." She clicked to the horse. "Let us find Lord Garrick. I need to rest for a bit and attend my needs. I would sell my soul for a garderobe in those woods ahead."

Melissa watched her parents interact. Her mind drifted to the conversations she had heard in the village concerning the new King and Queen. The country buzzed with colorful tales about Henry II—a rugged redhead with an unpredictable temper—and his beautiful, sophisticated consort, Eleanor of Aquitaine. Travelers who had seen them together declared it to be a love–match. This surprised no one considering the Queen's fascination with the Camelot legend and chivalry. Her troubadours were renowned for their romantic stories and songs about the knights of old.

Could there be passion and love for nobles? Did even the peasants and serfs have that luxury? No matter. Her lot had been drawn and she found herself excited at the thought of being lady of her own castle, mistress of her home. She dismounted on her own, ignoring the look from her mother, and waited to see which direction she and her maid went. Melissa purposely turned the other way.

The woods were dim with the day nearly at an end. They would not reach the next town before dark. She picked up her heavy skirts and walked farther into the trees; the quiet and solitude wrapped around her like a balm. Her horse followed behind, snatching at a random leaf that still clung to a branch. Common sense told her to turn around, but a noise—no, a song—floated over the stillness.

Without thought, Melissa moved toward the sound. She approached the edge of the forest and stopped just behind a large oak. A man stood on a hill beckoning to someone or something. His voice captured her, bound her to the spot, and her eyes fixed on the scene.

Silhouetted against the blood–orange sun sinking into the horizon, the dark, powerfully built figure slowly raised his right arm toward the evening sky. The sides of his mantle fluttered in the autumn breeze as a hawk screeched in answer. He raised his left arm and the howl of wolves echoed through the air in obedient response.

A sudden gust of air swirled the black, heavy cloak around the legs of the man, sending leaves flying about his feet as if they were commanded to dance. Melissa watched from behind the tree and held her breath, for fear of being discovered.

His resonant voice rose in a chant that captivated, then soothed. It spoke to her, beckoned her. She clutched at the rough tree bark to resist the physical pull. Then the chant abruptly ceased.

His head snapped around and tawny golden eyes locked onto hers. His gaze seemed to pierce her very soul, and her body pulsed in excitement as he pushed back the hood exposing raven hair and the chiseled features of an extraordinarily handsome face. She gasped, her gaze transfixed on the most magnificent creature she had ever seen.

Distant voices threatened to encroach upon this moment of fate. She pushed the sound to the back of her mind and focused only on the mysterious man in front of her. The urge to move closer overwhelmed her, and she stepped away from the shelter of the tree. Her feet moved of their own will, and her arms reached out to this stranger who now filled her with an intense need.

The voices behind her grew louder. Footsteps rustled dead leaves and brush, intruding on the enchantment. Her mind, not yet ready to let him go, struggled to stay in his world. But the mystical influence receded and she knew he had released his hold over her. An inexplicable emptiness took its place.

Melissa reluctantly turned towards the commotion behind her, certain he would be gone when she looked back over her shoulder. Would she see him again? Her father had spoken of a wizard rumored to have the ear of the king. Her mind a tangle of unexplained questions, she bowed her head and attempted a look of repentance as her father approached.

"Daughter! What were you thinking to wander off alone?" She heard more worry in his tone than anger. "These are hard times. I fear too many thieves lurk near the main roads."

"Yes, Milord." The relief on his face caused her to regret the impulse for a moment of privacy.

She cast one last glance toward the hill but spied only a single hawk, circling low. The bird landed on a nearby branch, observing the group. As Melissa admired its beauty, her heart raced. One hand covered her chest as her eyes locked onto a pair of golden ones. It cannot be him. Unless he is a...

The bird seemed to read her thoughts. With one sharp cry, the winged creature took flight and disappeared over the trees. She reached out to stop him, but he vanished into the night.

The travelers entered a small village that had already conceded to the winter. Tiny huts looked forlorn with any openings shuttered or covered with tanned animal skins. Thin tendrils of smoke drifted from the top of thatched roofs. The earl found an alehouse with respectable accommodations. Inside, a great fire roared in the open hearth and the smell of sizzling meat put the entire party in good humor.

Lord Garrick wiped the grease from his fingers and reached for a cup of wine. "Damned good venison. I think that may be the best meal we've had since we left home. With the coming of Advent, it will be a long while before we get more meat."

"Quality increases the closer we get to London. Though you don't care for fish, I am sure the dishes served at court will taste better than those from our kitchens." Lady Agnes pushed away her plate and patted her stomach. "Now if only we had a comfortable mattress."

Melissa stared into the fire. An ember popped and hit her skirt, shaking her from her thoughts. She brushed the cinder off and examined the tiny burn mark in the heavy wool. "Are wizards and magic real?"

"What?" Her father looked at her as if she had two heads, and then smirked. "I am certain of it. Watch me conjure up an evil spirit." He reached over and pinched his wife's bottom. She gave a yelp then began a torrent of reprimands. "See?"

"You tease me. I suppose it was a silly question."

"Daughter, you will see many wondrous things in the next month." He reached out and awkwardly patted her hand. "You shall make an excellent wife; your mother served you well."

Both women blushed at the praise. "Watch the festivities closely, especially the evening events," Agnes advised. "The Duke of Sunderland entertains often."

"Yes, milady." She reached in her pocket and felt the lemon balm leaves. With a little rub, the citrus scent drifted up, and she inhaled deeply.

"Are you nervous dear? That scent has calmed you since before you were born. I remember when your grandmother gave me the Melissa leaves to soothe me while I carried you. Afterward, I hoped the name would somehow impart a sense of tranquility and composure in your life." She winked at her husband. "She is composed, I suppose, but tranquil?"

Her parents' laughter faded when they saw Melissa's offended look.

Agnes squeezed her daughter's hand. "Take heart, my girl. This trip has been difficult but soon the excitement will begin."

"You are right. But at this moment, I only look forward to a good night of sleep," Melissa answered, returning their smile. "Mother, you must be tired too."

The older woman stifled a yawn. "Milord, with your permission, we ladies will retire. I believe you sent our traveling bags upstairs?"

"Yes, Agnes." He, too, let out a loud yawn and stretched his arms above his head. "I won't be long. I need to speak with my marshal and be sure the horses are well attended."

Melissa's maid had unpacked her night attire, and her pallet lay in front of a small fire crackling in the hearth. It always comforted her to know Beatrice was near. "Just a sneeze away," the older woman had told her since childhood. But neither her governess nor the lemon balm worked to relieve the tight ball in her stomach.

"Why can you not come with me?"

"You no longer need me, milady. You're all grown and soon to be mistress of your own home. It's only nerves, milady. Once you are settled, your duties will keep you so busy I will be an occasional thought." The older woman gently brushed Melissa's long blonde waves. "I love you like my own and will always be here when you need me." She pressed her hand over heart.

She gave Beatrice a hug. "I fear my mind is too full and will not rest. Help me to bed and sing to me until I fall asleep." The childhood melodies quieted her thoughts and her eyes closed.

Vivid dreams interrupted her slumber. She stood in small grove, shivering in the dark. She jumped at the sound of his voice.

"I have waited for you." The mysterious man on the hill stared at her from a tree.

"Come down right now," she commanded. Goosebumps prickled her arms, and she rubbed them with vigor. "How can you wait for me when we have never met?"

"You are my destiny."

"Ridiculous. You are neither man nor animal." Yet the blood rushing to her cheeks and the warmth that spread through her body said otherwise. He was indeed a man, whether he looked at her from under a hood or the eyes of a hawk. When she peered up at the tree again, he had vanished, and she cried out for him. Her skin chilled with his absence and her heart grew heavy.

"Please don't go. I would take back my harsh words."

A whisper tickled her ear, "We shall meet again."

Melissa sat bolt upright in bed. Her heart pounded as if she had run from the stables to the house. She clutched the damp shift to her chest and tried to catch her breath. Using the bed sheets to wipe the sweat from her face, she lay back down on the lumpy mattress.

What kind of sorcerer are you, and why do you invade my sleep? Leave me be.

But when she closed her lids, she knew golden eyes watched her from a distance. A soft, low chant lulled her back into a fitful slumber.

SNEAK PEEK

FOR THE LOVE OF LAURA BETH (A CHICAGO CHRISTMAS #4)

(Recreated from the previously published novella, Love's Challenge)

CHAPTER ONE

> *"Men always want to be woman's first love – women like to be a man's last romance."*

Oscar Wilde

April 1949

Sweet Grove, Texas

It was the kind of first kiss all girls dreamed of, hoped for, and rarely received. The kind of first kiss a girl saw in the movies or read in romance novels. The kind of first kiss a girl only whispered about because the moment was too precious to share.

A moment Laura Beth Walters had waited for almost ten years. She sighed and leaned her cheek into the hand that still cupped her face, afraid to open her eyes.

Joe put his forehead against hers. "So this is love."

Her lips still tingled from his touch. Her heart clamored against her chest. She wondered briefly if life would ever be this sweet again. Yes, this was love.

She'd known it since first grade, but Mom said boys were a bit slower in the cleverness department. She peeked through her lashes and looked into his deep chocolate eyes. His lids were half closed, and a sated smile played on his lips, as if he'd just tasted something heavenly. *Me*, she thought wickedly. The moon threw shadows across his strong jaw and square chin. He was the most handsome boy in Sweet Grove. No, in the entire state of Texas.

"Yes, Mr. McCall, I do believe it's love." She ran her fingertips down his cheek, the coarse, dark stubble bristly on her skin. Warmth spiraled through her with the intimate gesture. "What do you think?"

"I think I understand why my mom smiled at me, and my pa thumped me on the shoulder when I left tonight." Joe moved his hands around her waist, pulling her close. "So your parents will let you go to prom with a senior?"

Laura shrugged, trying for poise but failing miserably when the grin would not leave her face. Daddy had been reluctant to let her date. Her mother had come to the rescue, convincing him that sixteen was old enough to date a boy they trusted. The McCalls lived down the street and owned the local mechanic shop. Joe was a hardworking, polite boy. Their families attended neighborhood barbecues, community, and school functions together.

"I'm practically a senior."

"And Roger Willard will be practically comatose if he ever buys you another soda at the drugstore. I saw him giving you the eye last week." He leaned closer and whispered in her ear. "I don't know how I missed you growing up this past year, but I'm crazy about you now.

Their first date had come about by accident. She had been at Berkley's Pharmacy with a group of friends in late March. Tuesdays and Saturdays were her favorite days because Joe worked then. He looked so handsome in his white hat and jacket. Almost like a sailor or a doctor.

Laura had ordered a strawberry malt and was waiting for Joe to make it. He'd rubbed her head, still treating her like a child. "Give me minute, kid."

"I'll buy that," Roger said to Joe as he slid onto the stool next to her.

"Nah, I got it for her," Joe called over his shoulder.

"I *said* I'll buy Laura Beth the malt," Roger had repeated through clenched teeth.

Joe, a scowl on his face, had set the malt on the counter with a thud that made the other girls giggle. "Fine. Like I care who buys it for her."

But Joe had looked confused as he watched the other boy tip his head and talk to her. He studied Roger, then his childhood friend, and then looked at the boy as if something was definitely off. She knew the second it hit him, recognized the shock on his face.

"You're sweet on her. Sweet on my little Laura Beth." He shook his head and then looked at her again, as if for the first time.

"I'm done in here in half an hour. Wait for me," Joe said, with a narrow look at Roger.

"Sure, Joey. I'll wait," she'd said in her sweetest voice, and then continued to talk Roger.

Joe walked her home that day, rubbing his jaw and giving her odd looks as if she were the new girl in town. She swore he was mad at her for some reason.

When they reached her house, Laura had paused on the front steps.

"Are you okay?" she'd asked over her shoulder. "You're acting like an odd duck."

"Don't let Roger buy you any more malts." His voice came out gruff.

"Are you jealous?" A smile curled her lips.

"NO! Of course not, you're like my little sister." He pushed his hands in his jean pockets, his chin stuck out and a scowl on his face. "I mean, I've been lookin' out for you since we were kids."

"Well don't flip your wig. It was just a question." But something had changed, and her heart beat with the excitement of it. "See you tomorrow?"

"Nah, I gotta help Pa at the shop. I'll walk you to school on Monday." He peered at her from under his bushy brows. "I mean it about Roger, though."

And he walked away, kicking furiously at any rock in his path. Laura Beth squinted her eyes against the late afternoon sun and wondered if she'd finally been noticed.

The next week, an odd courtship began. Joe had always been popular with the girls so the possessiveness he displayed both thrilled her and created awkwardness between them. At any school activity, Joe appeared at her side. This also made the other boys looked at her differently. They began nodding at her or saying hello in the hall. Laura began dressing with care each morning and checking her image twice before entering the high school.

It took Joe a month to finally kiss her and then just a peck. They had stood on her front door step, the porch light on, when he bent down without warning and touched his lips to hers. Electricity shot through her. From the wonder in his eyes, Joe must have felt the same.

"I love you, Joe McCall," she had blurted out then slapped her hand over her mouth. Her skin had turned hot as the Rio Grande in summertime.

Then the door opened, her father towered over them, and the moment was over. Joe had walked away with a wink over his shoulder as Daddy held open the screen door, glowering. An arm around her at the theater, some handholding while they walked home, or a quick peck goodnight had been the extent of their closeness until tonight. After that, they were always in a group or with Joe's little brother, Leroy.

Now Laura Beth closed her eyes as his lips covered hers again. Her mother had been right. "A little healthy competition is good for the economy *and* love. Sometimes a man needs some help takin' off those blinders." Well, the blinders were certainly off. And the summer was just beginning.

***

August 1949
Sweet Grove Stop train station

"Now don't forget to call as soon as you get settled in. I need to know my boy is all right." Mrs. McCall pushed a stray lock of hair from her son's forehead. "Don't get in with those big city boys. Stay away from the girls with too much make-up and tight skirts."

"Dixie, the boy'll be fine. And he's got a nice little gal waitin' on him right here in Sweet Grove."

"You know I like Laura Beth, she's a sweet girl. But boys don't always marry their high school sweethearts." She patted Joe's cheek, her hazel eyes shining. "You just keep your options open."

"I didn't look any further than you, and we met my junior year in high school." He winked at his wife before turning back to Joe. "But your mother's right about the city. Only trust those who have earned it, and don't take everything at face value. "

"Yes, sir. I'll remember to keep my eyes open and mouth shut." Joe stuck out his hand, knowing his father was not the sentimental type. People said he was a younger version of his old man. But it had been more important to *be* like his father than look like him. Max McCall was bigger than life, and men respected him. Though 35, he'd enlisted after FDR announced the bombing of Pearl Harbor, leaving behind his ten-year-old son and wife. He'd come home to a defunct business, but he'd come home a hero.

His father grabbed him in a bear hug. "Sometimes a dang handshake just ain't enough."

Joe accepted a rare hug from his father, relieved they had moved past their disagreement over his career choice. McCall Motors was successful, but the thought of his head stuck under the hood of a car forever filled Joe with panic. Journalism, especially field reporting, had been under his skin since he listened to Edward R. Murrow's broadcasts as a kid. That news reporter was fearless. His commentary had brought the blitz of London into American living rooms. Pa had been fighting in Europe in 1942, and Murrow had been a lifeline of news and hope for the ten year old and his mother. With his no-nonsense, straight from the hip reporting, Joe swore the man had to be from Texas.

He hugged his mother again and saw Laura Beth half-running to the platform. She had dressed up for his departure in a pale blue sundress that matched her eyes and hugged her waist. The skirt flared over her round hips, swaying with each step. Her auburn waves brushed the collar of her short matching jacket that covered slender bare arms. His heart gave a little jump when those baby blues locked with his.

His proper little miss, who forgot all etiquette when she was near him. The past few months had been so sweet. If she could have fit in his suitcase, he might have tried to take her along. They had made grand plans for their future while they strolled the square on Saturday night or picnicked in the apple groves. Mr. Walters had even softened toward him a bit.

The whole thing was still a mystery to him. He'd always had a soft spot for the little girl who gazed at him with adoration. She was a nuisance, but he'd felt protective over her just the same. One day she was the kid down the street, and then —wham!—the next, she'd claimed his heart.

"Joey, I was afraid I'd miss you." Laura Beth threw her arms around his neck, and he picked her up off the ground, swinging her in a wide circle. "What will I ever do without you until Thanksgiving? Austin seems like it's on the other side of the world."

Back on her feet, she noticed his parents behind him and turned an adorable pink. "Mr. and Mrs. McCall, I beg your pardon. I'm just so...so—"

"No need to apologize, darlin'. We understand. He'll be sorely missed around here." His father put an arm around Laura's shoulder and squeezed. "Besides, you're my savior. If you hadn't promised to take Joe's place at Sunday service with my wife, I'd have to go. And those long, boring sermons are made for napping but the darn wooden benches sure aren't."

His wife smacked his arm with a gloved hand. "Don't listen to my heathen of a husband, sugar. I appreciate the company."

"Leroy! Leroy, get over here and tell your brother goodbye." Dixie pushed back a strawberry blonde wave behind her ear, waving her youngest son away from the train. "Don't you try to sneak on there. You're father will whoop your hide if we have to go to Austin and pick you up."

The freckled four-year-old came running, his hands stuffing something in his bulging pockets. He saw Laura Beth and jumped at her, his arms slung around her neck.

"Hi bewtiful," he said, mimicking his big brother.

"Leroy," his mother admonished, "dump those rocks out right now. You are not bringing any more into the house."

He shook his head frantically and buried his head in Laura's neck. His hair, though the same color as his mother's, was a mass of curls that Dixie refused to cut. Right now, they were plastered to his freckled face.

"They's pwetty ones, Mama. Some a dem have spawkles like Lawa Bef's eyes." He grinned at her now and gave her a kiss on the cheek before wriggling down.

Then he made the same leap at Joe. "Wuv you, Joey. I'll watch out for Lawa Bef."

The train whistle blew, and Joe hugged his little brother to him before the boy wriggled and jumped down. Then he looked at the two most important women in his life. He prayed they would become good friends while he was away. His father put out his hand for one last shake, his mother gave him a final hug, and he stole one more kiss from his girl in front of God and anyone who cared to watch.

"Ew, now ya gotta get mawied."

About the Author

Bestselling and award-winning author Aubrey Wynne resides in the Midwest with her husband, dogs, horses, mule and barn cats. She is an elementary teacher by trade, champion of children and animals by conscience, and author by night. Obsessions include history, travel, trail riding and all things Christmas.

Her short stories, ***Merry Christmas, Henry and Pete's Mighty Purty Privies*** have won Readers Choice Awards. ***Dante's Gift*** and ***Paper Love*** received the 2016 Golden Quill, Aspen Gold, Heart of Excellence and the Gayle Wilson Award of Excellence.

In addition to her Chicago Christmas novellas, Aubrey will release two more Regency romances in 2018. The Wicked Earls' Club will release again in 2019. Wynne's medieval fantasy series launched in 2017 with ***Rolf's Quest***, winner of the NTRWA Great Expectations.

Also by Aubrey Wynne

A Chicago Christmas series

Dante's Gift
(A Chicago Christmas #1)

http://aubreywynne.com/book/dantes-gift-a-chicago-christmas-1/
Winner of the Golden Quill and Heart of Excellence RWA awards

"Wynne has crafted a a beautiful short story guaranteed to warm your heart and make you sigh."

Kishan Paul, Second Wife Series

"...a wonderfully poignant holiday romantic tale that intertwines two love stories..."

Jersey Girls Book Reviews

"A lovely sweet romance!"

Book Addicts

Kathleen James has put her practical side away for once and looks forward to the perfect romantic evening: an intimate dinner with the man of her dreams—and an engagement ring. She is not prepared to hear that he wants to bring his grandmother back from Italy to live with him.

Dominic Lawrence has planned this marriage proposal for six months. Nothing can go wrong— until his Nonna calls. Now he must interrupt the tenderest night of Katie's life with the news that another woman will be under their roof.

When Antonia's sister dies, she finds herself longing to be back in the states. An Italian wartime bride from the '40s, she knows how precious love can be. Can her own story of an American soldier and a very special collie once again bring two hearts together at Christmas?

Paper Love
(A Chicago Christmas #2)

http://aubreywynne.com/book/paper-love-a-chicago-christmas-2/

Bragg Medallion recipient, Winner of Gayle Wilson Award for Excellence, Golden Quill and Aspen Gold finalist

"This author has a knack for love stories that make your heart flutter."

Reads2Love Book Reviews

"Aubrey Wynne is a talented author weaving a descriptive setting, cultural details, historical facts, and inspirational romance into a delightful read."

Renate, Goodreads Review

Growing up in a Papua New Guinea mission, Joss Palmateer is a gentle soul with a unique view of life. Still adjusting to a new home in the U.S and the sudden loss of her mother, love is the last thing on her mind.

Sexy physical therapist, Ben Montgomery, meets his sister's friend and the sparks fly. He takes it as a silent challenge when she ignores his advances, but it's her extraordinary inner beauty that captures his heart.

With the help of a stray homing pigeon and an old origami legend, Ben sets an unwavering course of romance to win her love.

MERRY CHRISTMAS, HENRY
(A CHICAGO CHRISTMAS #3)
http://aubreywynne.com/book/merry-christmas-henry-a-chicago-christmas-3/
Preditors and Editors Readers Choice Award

"Captivating Christmas Choice!"

Kindle Book Review

"Short, sweet, and stunning!"

Great Reads

Henry, a shy and talented artist, moonlights as a security guard at a museum and loses his heart to a beautiful, melancholy woman in a painting. As his obsession grows, he finds a kindred soul who helps him in his search for happiness. On Christmas Eve, Henry dares to take a chance on love and fulfill his dream.

Regency Romance

Earl of Sunderland
(Wicked Earl series)
(Once Upon a Widow prequel)
http://aubreywynne.com/book/earl-of-sunderland/

"Well-written historical romance with a bit of everything – a tragedy, a conflicted hero, a strong and fragile heroine, interesting characters, and a happily ever after."

Amazon verified review

"Best Regency Romance I've read in a long time and highly recommend!"

N.N. Light Book Heaven Reviews

"I adored this story. I look forward to reading more in this series."

Reads2Love Review

"A wonderful romance!"

5 Kindles Review

Grace Beaumont has seen what love can do to a woman. Her mother sacrificed her life to produce the coveted son and heir. A devastated father and newborn brother force her to take on the role of Lady Boldon at the age of fifteen. But Grace finds solace in the freedom and power of her new status.

Christopher Roker made a name for himself in the military. The rigor and pragmatism of the army suits him. When a tragic accident heaves Kit into a role he never wanted or expected, his world collides with another type of duty. Returning to England and his newfound responsibilities, the Wicked Earls' Club becomes a refuge from the glitter and malice of London society but cannot ease his emptiness.

Needing an escape from his late brother's memory and reputation, Kit visits the family estate for the summer. Lady Grace, a beauty visiting from a neighboring estate, becomes a welcome distraction. When the chance to return to the military becomes a valid possibility, the earl finds himself wavering between his old life and the lure of an exceptional—and unwilling—woman.

COMING SOON:
A WICKED EARL'S WIDOW
(ONCE UPON A WIDOW #1)
http://aubreywynne.com/book/a-wicked-earls-widow/

When Eliza's abusive father forced her into marriage, she had no idea her life would change for the better. Married less than a year, her unwilling rake of a husband had been surprisingly kind to her—until his sudden death. The widowed Countess of Sunderland is more than happy to remain with her in-laws and raise their daughter. Unfortunately, her own family is on the brink of financial ruin and has other plans.

Nathaniel, Viscount of Pendleton, gained his title at the age of 12. His kindly but astute estate manager became father and mentor, instilling in the boy an astute sense of responsibility and compassion for his tenants. Fifteen years later, his family urges him to visit London and seek a wife. The ideal doesn't appeal to him, but his sense of duty tells him it is the next logical step.

When Lord Pendleton stumbles upon Eliza on the road, defending an elderly woman against ruffians, he's shocked and intrigued. After rescuing the exquisite damsel in distress, he finds himself smitten. But Nate soon realizes he must discover the dark secrets of her past to truly save the woman he loves.

Rhapsody and Rebellion
(Once Upon a Widow #2)
(Enduring Legacy #7)
http://aubreywynne.com/book/rhapsody-and-rebellion/

An enduring legacy... A rebellion... A destined love...

Raised in his father's image—practical and disciplined—there are no gray lines interrupting the Earl of Stanfeld's black and white world. Until his mother has a dream and begs to return to her Highland home.

Alisabeth was betrothed from the cradle. At seventeen, she marries her best friend and finds happiness if not passion. In less than a year, she's a widow. Vowing to honor her husband's memory, she joins his activist group of Glasgow weavers and is soon embroiled in the Radical War of 1820.

Crossing the border into Scotland, Gideon finds his predictable world turned upside down. Folklore, legend, and political unrest intertwine with an unexpected attraction to a feisty Highland beauty. But Lissie doesn't trust the Englishman or the rising desire between them. When the earl learns of an English plot to stir the Scots into rebellion, he must choose his country or save the clan and the woman that stirs his soul.

ROLF'S QUEST
(A MEDIEVAL ENCOUNTER #1)
http://aubreywynne.com/aubreys-books/aubreys-historical-romance/
Great Expectations winner, Fire & Ice finalist, Maggie finalist

"Author Aubrey Wynne brings a swashbuckling epic story of family, love and betrayal to life in "Rolf's Quest". The structure of the story is done well -- it is long on action and moves at breakneck speed. The plot is perfectly paced, with characters that will pull the reader right into the action. They are likable and readers will root for Rolf and Melissa throughout their struggles. The strength of their bond will keep readers glued to their seat right until the very last page. Hold onto your helmet, readers, and grab a shield -- Rolf is just around the corner."

InD'tale magazine

"This was a surprisingly smooth read that I flew through in practically one sitting. I loved how easily I was immersed in this medieval world filled with royalty, knights, wizards, and villains. The magical element was interesting and I liked the way Merlin's story was woven into this book. The plot sucked me in and I thoroughly enjoyed following Rolf's journey.

In closing... A story with pretty much everything a fantasy romance fan can want. 4.5 stars"

Romance Reviews

A wizard, a curse, a fated love...

When Rolf finally discovers the woman who can end the curse that has plagued his family for centuries, she is already betrothed. Time is running out for the royal wizard of King Henry II. If he cannot find true love without the use of sorcery, the magic will die for future generations.

Melissa is intrigued by the mystical, handsome man who haunts her by night and tempts her by day. His bizarre tale of Merlin, enchantments, and finding genuine love has her questioning his sanity and her heart.

From the moment Melissa stepped from his dreams and into his arms, Rolf knew she was his destiny. Now, he will battle against time, a powerful duke, and call on the gods to save her.

Small Town Romance series
Saving Grace
(A Small Town Romance #1)

http://aubreywynne.com/smalltown-romance/

"This unique piece has the reader traveling between the early 1700s and the early 2000s with ease and amazement. The audience truly feels sorrow for Grace and Chloe and is able to connect with each woman for the hardships they are overcoming. The attention to historical facts and details leave one breathless especially upon learning the people from the past did exist and the memorial erected still stands."

InD'Tale Magazine

"I enjoyed the way the book went from past to present really pulling the read in. The mystery was a delight. The author gives a wonderful story of two women fighting to keep what is theirs, showing their strength, love and courage to put one foot in front of the other while the world around them goes crazy."

Cyn, Top 500 Reviewer

A tortured soul meets a shattered heart...

Chloe Hicks' life consisted of an egocentric ex-husband, a pile of bills, and an equine business in foreclosure until a fire destroys the stable and her beloved ranch horse. What little hope she has left is smashed after the marshal suspects arson. She escapes the accusing eyes of her hometown, but not the memories and melancholy.

Jackson Hahn, Virginia Beach's local historian, has his eyes on the mysterious new woman in town. When she enters his office, he is struck by her haunting beauty and the raw pain in her eyes. Her descriptions of the odd events happening in her bungalow pique his curiosity.

The sexy historian distracts Chloe with the legend of a woman wrongly accused of witchcraft. She is drawn to the story and the similarities of events that plagued their lives. Perhaps the past can help heal the present. But danger lurks in the shadows...

FOR THE LOVE OF LAURA BETH
(SMALL TOWN ROMANCE #2)

"Beautifully written and tells a story that will allow readers to experience the turmoil that war can bring to the lives of those who must endure its heartbreak."

Amazon Review

"This isn't your typical boy-meets-girl-they-get-married-and-live-happily-ever-after-the-end story. This is sweet romance in the midst of real life hardships and pain, and a love that will press through and triumph."

Amazon Review

The Korean War destroyed their plans, but the battle at home may shatter their hearts...

Laura Beth Walters fell in love with Joe McCall when she was six years old. Now she is counting the days until Joey graduates from college so they can marry and begin their life together. But the Korean War rips their neatly laid plans to shreds. Instead of a college fraternity, Joey joins a platoon. Laura Beth trades a traditional wedding for a quick trip to the courthouse.

They endure the hardship of separation, but the true battle is faced when Joey returns from the war. Their marriage is soon tested beyond endurance. Joe and Laura Beth must find a way to accept the trials thrown in their path or lose the love that has kept them anchored for so long.

Just for Sh*#$ and Giggles series
To Cast A Cliche
(A Just for Sh*#$ and Giggles Short Story #1)

http://aubreywynne.com/book/to-cast-a-cliche/

"...a fractured fairy tale with humor and tongue in cheek...to use a cliché."

Amazon Reviewer

"Fairy tale lovers will delight in this short story... It's a fun read that will have you playing "count the cliches" until the cows come home."

Reads2Love

The evil Queen Lucinda exacts revenge on a royal poet by casting a spell of never-ending clichés upon the kingdom. Will the clever King Richard thwart his stepmother's magic and save the good people of Maxim? Test your literary knowledge and enjoy an entertaining spoof on fairytales.

Pete's Mighty Purty Privies
(A Just for Sh*#$ and Giggles Short Story #2)

http://aubreywynne.com/book/petes-mighty-purty-privies/

***Preditor's and Editors Readers Choice
Award***
Goodread's Top 100 Laugh Out Loud List

"The author has a gift for clarity and humor and I can't recommend this short story enough. Hilarious!"

N.N. Light Book Reviews

"Expertly written and hysterical. You can't go wrong with this one."

Renea Mason, The Good Doctor trilogy

Pete McNutt needs customers for his new business. Spring has arrived and it's prime time Privy Season. After much consideration, he refines his sales pitch and heads to the monthly meeting of the Women's Library Association.

Made in the USA
San Bernardino, CA
29 November 2018